love *Sophie Soames* London 2024

DIRTY SEXY STUPID LOVE

SOPHIA SOAMES

Rourke xo

2024
RARE
EDINBURGH
EXCLUSIVE

Signed with *love*

Linktr.ee/Rourke

Paperback ISBN: 9798399501420

Hardcover ISBN: 9798873824847

ASIN: B0C6QFK64F

Cover Design © 2023 Sophia Soames

Cover Model/Photographer Rourke Ely Linktr.ee/rourke

All images, artwork and fonts are licensed for commercial use by Sophia Soames, for distribution via electronic media and/or print. Final copy and promotional rights included.

Editing by Debbie McGowan

Proofreading by Sarah Coppin

Sensitivity reader Vin George

Formatting by K.C. Carmine

Summary

In the weeks leading up to his best friend's wedding, twenty-three-year-old Harry Thunder truly hits rock bottom. Existing in a haze of vodka and self-destruction, there's more to Harry's obnoxious behaviour than meets the eye.

But life, as he knows it, is about to change, and not even Harry can stop the tsunami of feelings when he finally realises that he's allowed to be happy. That he's just as loveable as people like...Owen Cartwright.

Owen is large and loud and calls everyone babes, while Harry can't even string a coherent sentence together, let alone get through the day without life punching him in the face.

But perhaps sometimes being exactly who you are can be why people fall in love with you.

Even if you're not gay. At all.

author's note

E metophobia is an extreme fear of vomiting, seeing vomit, watching other people vomit, or even feeling sick. It can affect people in lots of different ways, but if you think you may be struggling with emetophobia, you are not alone - and should probably skip the end of chapter one.

Content warnings for alcoholism, assault, really bad parenting, homophobia and mentions of bullying.

■

chapter one

Harry

The asphalt smashing into my skull came as no surprise, neither did the hard wet ground slapping against my throbbing skin as my head bounced around like a football. I somehow managed to lift it high enough to spit some metallic-tasting foam from my mouth as my arms cradled around my face in an attempt at protection. Nope, no surprise, I kid you not. I'd seen it coming since I'd thrown a drink across the bar, somewhere towards that dude with the stupid smirk, and another guy had shouted at me to take it outside and show him I meant business. Not the best end to the evening, but I hadn't wanted to stay in that shitty place anyway. Some posh gay club with blokes in cages and overpriced drinks. Not that I cared about the blokes. But the company had been well below par, and nobody was interested in the drunk hurling abuse at anyone who would listen.

Yes, that had been me. Again. Too drunk to be served, apparently. It wasn't the first time and wouldn't be the last, and the familiar feeling of dread and shame was creeping in, making the hairs on the back of my neck stand on end. I needed another drink.

I hadn't changed a bit, despite my ego telling me I'd morphed into some kind of responsible grown-up. A better man. A human being who showed empathy and care for the humans around me. I'd not become my dad.

Except I had. It hurt to admit it, every time. I was no better than anyone else. I was still a complete tool, a selfish idiot, a dickhead and a drunk—all traits my father would have encouraged and which I'd perfected with some kind of misguided pride in being my father's son. There was blood pooling in my mouth, and I clumsily spat it out, smearing the grit off the ground over my lips in the process.

So here I was, face down in the dirt, and my cheek was throbbing from the fist that had landed dangerously close to my eye. It didn't help that the owner of that fist was now standing over me, hurling abuse at my sorry arse. And my face. And my kneecap. The pavement had done some serious damage to my inebriated body, and I winced as another well-placed kick hit my hip. He wasn't done with me yet, and I didn't blame him. I'd called him some goddamn ugly words, and I suppose ridiculing his girlfriend's outfit right in front of him hadn't been one of my brighter ideas, especially since I was out on a stag do with a bunch of people who were supposed to be my best friends.

Best friends. What a juvenile thing to say. I had no friends. These were acquaintances at best, a bunch of lads I'd once shared classrooms with at senior school. People who had been idiotic nerds back then and were stupidly successful idiots now. I'd been successful back then, in a way. Now I wasn't, which meant that when I spent time with them, I ended up like this. The idiot who inevitably drank too much, did stupid shit, said even stupider things and ended up in the gutter.

At least I could joke about it—how I envied them, these people who were supposed to have been the bottom dwellers in life and had instead taken up all the top spots, leaving me to trail around behind them like a fool. In reality, I hated them all. Detested them and their perfect lives and happy engagements and bloody new sofas and...and... Those kinds of thoughts always brought out the worst in me.

I spat another gobful of saliva onto the ground, scraping my chin against the pavement. I'd look like shit in the morning, but I was too drunk to care. My mind was floating in a vodka-infused haze, and somewhere behind the ringing in my ears and the throbbing pain in my hip and my bruised knee and mangled face, I could hear laughter. In my younger days, that would have brought me to my feet with my fists up ready to fight.

I didn't think I had it in me to fight anymore. I should have been getting up and taking on whoever had just placed another well-aimed kick in my thigh, but I felt like giving up, just lying here and letting myself hurt. At least that way, I felt something I could put a label on. The pain was becoming the perfect blend in my head when someone grabbed hold of my jacket and tried to get me on my feet.

"Bloody hell, Harry."

There was no care in that voice. Just disappointment. I knew that voice better than I knew myself. Eddie Sumner. Idiot number one. The guy I'd known since we were both in nappies.

I laughed, but it sounded more like a whine.

"Are you going to lie here and let those bastards kick you to death?" Eddie again. He'd gone off to uni and had a career. A glittering future. "Let me get you up. Come on, mate."

"Yoouu..." I tried to speak, but something was wrong with my tongue.

"You're pissed, Harry. Again. And you got into a fight. Again." He sounded tired and pissed off. I would have been disappointed in myself too. "It's our stag night, and you promised!"

I had. And I'd let him down. There was obviously something wrong with me. Something Eddie never failed to remind me of.

"You need to stop this. The drinking is out of hand—the fact that you can't stay out of trouble, just for one night... You promised, mate. You promised!"

Lectures. And here was Joe. Idiot number two. Also, Eddie's husband-to-be. They'd met at school and had stuck to each other like bloody magnets ever since. Eddie had been in my year. Joe in the year below.

"You're...youure...You're not supposed to be here. It's a...schtagdoo."

"Where's Owen when you need him?" Joe sighed, grabbed my other arm and slung it around his shoulders. He was still as skinny as he'd been back in school. Skinny and weird, full of angles and long black curls. He needed a haircut, which I tried to tell him, but it came out as bubbles with added weird sounds.

"It's a joint stag do, Harry. We keep telling you."

I wanted to remind him that it wasn't healthy for him and Eddie to be joined at the hip all the time. He could have gone out with his other mate, this Owen whatever, and let Eddie have his own stag do. I was the best man...or supposed to be. I wasn't so sure anymore. I'd been threatened with demotion from that role several times this evening, and Eddie was kind of scary when he was mad—something I had so easily forgotten but was reminded of now, as he and Joe manhandled me up some stairs only to be shouted at by someone in a hi-viz jacket whose name was Security. At least, that's what it said on the twat's name badge. I tried to point this out to Eddie, but this Security was telling me I was barred, and Eddie was shouting too, I think...

"You are such a dick, Harry! Any minute, the police will turn up. You didn't need to do this! Not this time. Not today."

"The future's school bright, man...we've gotta wear shaaades!"

That was my go-to line. The one that used to make Eddie smile. Now he stared at me in disgust. "Come on, lighten up!"

He didn't lighten up. Just sighed and tried to keep me upright.

Right on cue, there he was, Owen. Joe's mate from work. Built like a brick wall, hairy and furry like some oversized teddy bear. He should have been a rugby player.

"Oweeeen!" I squealed out. "Man, you schouuuld have been a...a...lugby player..."

He may have looked terrifying, but Owen was anything but. He loved everyone, or everyone except me. He hated my guts, mostly because Eddie tended to assign me into Owen's care, like I needed a babysitter. I obviously couldn't be trusted to look after myself when we all went out, and it wasn't the first time I had been picked up by the waist by this...monster...and carried down stairs. Next minute, I'd get thrown into the gutter again and get a matching bruise on my currently un-bruised cheek. Not that I didn't deserve it. I did.

He shouldn't have tried to carry me, though. His thick, furry arms squeezed the life out of me as he set me down on my feet, but there was something wrong with my legs. They were shaking like jelly, unsteady and weak, and if Owen hadn't squeezed me again, I would have fallen flat on my face. I tried to giggle, but I was suddenly retching violently.

"Don't," I said, but too late. Owen's arm was around my stomach, and now I was regurgitating a nightful of vodka right onto the pavement, where I'd be spending the night. No taxi would ever agree to take me home now.

I didn't even know why I was considering going home. I hated the four walls that masqueraded as my abode—the house I had grown up in, where my mother and father had spent most of my childhood in ice-cold anger. It was just me left now. My mother had relocated to Tenerife, and my father had had a massive heart attack on my twenty-third birthday. He'd gifted me the forever absence of his presence in my life. And his bankrupt business and our former home. An empty house with no soul.

No wonder I drank. I tried to explain this to Owen as he held me, stooped forward with vomit on my shoes. My mouth was still running even though my brain was stuck in fog.

"I hate that...housche. And...you're...you're all gay." Yeah. That was the way I usually riled Owen up. Pointing out the obvious.

"Babes." He sighed.

"Shodda..." I drooled, and another fresh batch of regurgitated cocktails hit the gutter in front of me. If Owen hadn't been holding me up, I would have face-planted straight into it...and been run over by the taxi that had just pulled up in front of us.

"Whyddya always go to gay clubs," I eloquently continued. I was an idiot, and I knew it.

"Harry, just shut up and pretend you're conscious. Here, wipe your mouth, babes. Don't want you stinking out the car for the poor driver."

"You're..." I was going to say something else, another stupid put down or whatever I could think of to make him talk to me. This was my usual show. Any normal person would have just grabbed hold of a mate and admitted they'd had too much to drink. They might even have admitted they were shit scared of being alone, didn't want to go home, did all this crap for attention. But because I was an insecure twat with issues, I did this. This...I couldn't even get my brain to work hard enough to find words for my behaviour.

I did this...because...because when I got like this? I would suddenly find myself exactly where I needed to be. Where my body would calm and my head would go into that place where I could finally breathe. It made no sense. None at all.

"You got this?" Eddie again, opening the car door so Owen could shove my sorry arse onto the back seat. "Here, sickbag." Trust Eddie Sumner to still care about my obvious need for something to contain the contents of my stomach. More likely he cared about the high possibility of Owen's trousers getting ruined.

"I'll call you later," I heard Owen say. Then there were hugs. Soft kisses against lips. Friendships. Not the kind of friendships I'd ever had. These were lifelong friendships. Mutual respect. Affection and hugs. Dare I say it? Love.

I told you I was green with envy. These were all things that someone like me would never have. I didn't deserve them. Never would.

"Fucking gays," I muttered under my breath as Owen slammed the door shut. Instead I had this.

"Oh, Harry." Owen leaned over to fasten my seat belt like I was a child. I opened my mouth to say something else, but nothing came out. Just empty puffs of stale air.

"You know we all love you," Owen said quietly, leaving his hand on my arm in a small gesture of comfort.

I pushed him away. "I'm not gay."

"Of course you're not," Owen replied. "Of course you're not."

chapter two

Owen

It wasn't the thin strips of sun streaming through the blinds that woke me up. Nor was it the car thundering down the road. No, it was an overwhelming fear, one I had started to recognise. He was still here, and thank God for that. I couldn't bear the thought of him having got up and headed out, not in the state he'd been in. I'd woken up a few times during the night, gently reaching out to make sure he was still there, his skin reassuringly hot to the touch.

My heart, which had skipped a few beats while my hand searched for him, was now returning to its slow, steady rhythm. Harry Thunder was alive and breathing, his dirty-blonde hair spread over the pillow next to me. A blushing bruise had taken shape across his freckled cheek, the skin blooming dark under his eye. Harry had been gaunt and pale as long as I'd known him, but now he looked positively unwell against my white sheets.

"You're staring at me again," he muttered.

Oh, so he was awake. I thought he'd been, but you never could tell. His breathing was quiet and shallow, even when fast asleep. I knew him better than I should have, but that was just the way it was.

"Of course I am. You've stolen all the duvet again. You thief."

I was going for light-hearted, and it raised a tiny smile—one which was quickly replaced with a grimace. His face must've ached, all swollen and bruised.

"As long as we didn't cuddle. Please tell me we didn't."

That was our usual joke.

"Your virtue is perfectly intact, Mr Thunder. I give you my word. You even showered once we got here, and put on pants. Very civilised of you, by the way."

"Jezus." He huffed, pulling covers tighter under his chin, still not opening his eyes.

"You feeling OK? How's your head?" I leant over so I could get a better look at his mangled lip.

"You tell me, you're the goddamn medic."

"Nurse, thank you very much, and I'm sorry to say, you look like shit. You could have lost an eye and gotten yourself killed, babes!" I wasn't being overdramatic. It was true, he could have. "At this rate, you will actually get yourself into some truly dangerous situation and do some serious damage to yourself. And no doubt endanger your friends. Can you sit up? Please? I'm just going to touch your face to check for fractures. Any dizziness? Visual disturbance? There's a bucket on the floor, please don't barf in the bed, babes."

"Sorry about...you know. It won't happen again," he said gingerly.

"You said that last time." I was supposed to be nice and caring here. The supportive friend. But my patience was starting to wear thin.

"It won't." He wouldn't look at me, despite me holding his chin up and carefully examining his bloodshot eyes.

"That's what you said after Eddie's birthday party. And Joe's birthday party. And Eddie's mum's work-do, and that Halloween party, not to mention Christmas and New Year's. You stayed here for three days that time, Harry, because you couldn't even walk."

"I'd just buried my dad, arsehole."

"I know, babes, but still."

"You said I could stay."

"I couldn't get rid of you."

"You're the one who always drags me back here, when you could just send me home in a taxi."

"I'd never send you home in a taxi. My weekends wouldn't be the same without you camping out in my bed."

He smiled, grimaced and lay back down, covering his face with his hand. "How bad is it?" His voice sounded small. Frightened.

"You'll live."

"Thanks."

"You look like you've been run over by a truck."

"Lucky I don't have a job to go to anymore, then."

I didn't even reply to that little sly attempt at guilt-tripping me. Just sat back and arranged the pillows behind my back.

He would have been a handsome man with a little bit of sunshine on his cheeks and nutrition in his body. While he'd always been skinny and grey, he looked worse than ever, something that filled me with unease. As his friends, we should have done something sooner, not just let him slide like this. Not that I was his friend. He was Eddie and Joe's dickhead mate, the one who had somehow stuck around like a bad smell.

The first time I'd met him—this guy who'd once apparently tormented everyone at school, a twat of the highest degree and someone I should have avoided like the plague—I'd been looking out for someone tall and terrifying, a textbook bully with bulk and presence. Instead, I remembered grabbing Joe in the kitchen, asking who the little twink in the corner was. The one who could barely look at anyone and whose leg kept jumping in nervous unease. Joe had rolled his eyes and sighed. Harry's bark was way bigger than his bite, and despite my reservations, he'd become part of our little team of grown-up misfits. Because when Harry was in a good mood and sober, he was a completely different person. Eddie kept him in line, while Joe rolled his eyes at his lame comebacks, and once the board games came out, Harry settled into his comfort zone. If I hadn't known any better, I would have fallen head over heels in love with him over that first night of Monopoly and KFC at Eddie and Joe's housewarming a year ago. How had it been a year?

I sighed, probably a little too loudly, as Harry rolled over, dragging the duvet off my legs. That last bit had been a blatant lie. I *had* fallen head over heels in love with him from that very first evening.

"Coffee?" I offered, even though I didn't want to get up. I could easily have rolled over and gone back to sleep, but now I was awake, the usual turbulence of feelings had kicked in.

"Yeah," he mumbled into the pillow.

"Rude!" I sneered at his back. He didn't reply.

It was calming, the slow ritual of making coffee, something to do with my hands in my little kitchen. I'd bought this house a year ago, a small newbuild starter home, a little over my budget, but it had been worth every penny.

When I'd first met Joe at nursing college, we'd bonded over having grown up in the same dead-end town, sharing stories of familiar places, though never having crossed paths. He'd been a constant in my life ever since, the weird-looking guy with the rainbow pin on his lapel and a smile that could melt ice caps. He'd let me mother him and follow him around, and never once had he told me to piss off despite my obvious crush on his very handsome boyfriend. Gosh. Eddie Sumner. Handsome bastard. All gym body and dimples and perfect hair. Nicest guy ever, though, and...well, the guy only had eyes for Joe. Eddie still teased me about my obvious infatuation, and in return, I never failed to pay him all the compliments. Joe kept saying Eddie's head would explode if I didn't calm down with the fangirling around his husband-to-be. His friend Kim thought it was the funniest thing ever. I got over it, of course I did, but I still couldn't help giving his arms a little squeeze whenever he was near. He had biceps to die for. Shoulders that just begged to be drooled over, and yeah. He knew it. So did Joe, who was lucky enough to get to do whatever he wanted to that body of his...

Enough with the dirty thoughts. I looked out the windows at the dim view across the street, the cathedral tower just about visible in the distance. I'd never thought I'd come back here once I'd headed off to college, but growing up did strange things to your plans, and once Joe and I'd both got our qualifications, home had been the obvious place to go. Joe was a trauma nurse in A&E at Medway Hospital, and I'd followed him, joining the surgical team there a few months later. Uni had been good for Eddie too, and he now headed up the sales team at some big IT set-up in town. The two of them had bought a house and were getting married; all they needed was the Volvo, two point four children and some mongrel of a dog and the fairy tale would be complete.

As for me... Ugh. I was an only child, and now a single gay man. In the queer community, looks were everything, and for an oversized brick of a man like me, with not a hint of muscle tone and a face that only a mother could love, I couldn't even boast about having a giant dick on Grindr. (I was obviously endowed with an average-sized handsome piece of equipment, but in Grindr terms, it was nothing to write home about.)

At least I still had a good mop of brownish hair on my head. I supposed I could have promoted myself as some kind of bear, since I was kind of big and hairy, but no. I was single and unwanted and had given up on getting laid. The only time I got remotely close to a dick that wasn't mine was when the dickhead currently in my bed decided to get too drunk and disorderly to make it home under his own steam.

"Want toast?" I shouted, hoping he'd be cooperative in at least getting some carbs into that stomach of his. I'd even bought white bread, especially, knowing that going out with Harry in tow would mean having him warm my bed for the weekend, and I meant that in a completely nonsexual way. Harry was straight, although his antics in the pulling department had been seriously lacking, and I couldn't remember ever seeing him get down with anyone, let alone show interest. Unless he was drunk when, instead of getting laid, he got into fights.

I buttered some toast for Harry and poured a bowl of muesli for myself. I was trying to lose weight, honestly. I'd started numerous diets over the last year, much to Joe's disgust.

"You just need to be yourself, Owen," he'd say, tutting at me pulling in my stomach in front of the mirror. I wore loose scrubs for work, but I'd bought a suit a size too small, aiming to look a million dollars for Joe and Eddie's wedding. I'd be going in a tracksuit at this rate, especially with Harry in my bed, eyeing up the toast with a green tinge forming on his cheeks. I was eyeing up that toast myself. I could have killed for a buttery croissant. Preferably smothered in jam.

"Eat," I said sternly.

"Yes, Mother," he sighed back.

He did eat, while I stuffed my mouth with muesli, trying to think of something to say that would make the guy next to me talk. He was a ball of nervous energy, a roaring fire churning in that stomach of his. There were things going on that he obviously didn't want to talk about, and my heart bled for anyone standing in his way once he tipped over the edge. I had no doubt he was brewing like a grenade and dealing with things that would at some point properly blow that fuse inside of him.

"Babes?" I started but said nothing more, unable to find the right words.

"I don't want to talk about it." Standard answer. We'd been here before.

"You know, you don't have to do whatever you're doing on your own."

"I'm not. You were all out necking drinks last night. I was with you lot, and whatever I do is my business. Don't stick your beak in stuff just for the sake of it."

He was slurring slightly, spilling crumbs onto the sheets. He took a slurp of his coffee and hissed as the hot liquid hit his tongue. "You trying to kill me?" He only narrowly avoided spilling it, and my heart once again skipped a beat as he turned to me with a mischievous grin. "I know how much you love your *lovely cream* carpet."

"Don't be a dick." I was sulking. This wasn't what I wanted. I wanted him to talk to me. Properly. I wanted words, feelings. Most of all, I wanted to know what on earth I could do to make all of this stop.

"This isn't a hook-up," I snarled. "You don't have to even pretend that you like me. Just be fucking nice."

"Thank God for that! Someone has to be straight in this town."

I shrugged. "Not my fault that you hang around a bunch of queers. And anyway, Kim and Ella are straight."

"I have other friends, you know."

He was lying, I could always tell. There was something in his mannerisms that changed when he wasn't telling the truth—another little thing I kind of liked about Harry Thunder. He was so easy to read. Like an open book. Like when he tried to blink and bit his lip, thinking I wouldn't notice. He was in pain.

I handed him the two pills I'd prepared earlier. "Ibuprofen. For the swelling, and it will help with the pain too."

"Thank you, Nurse."

We sat there in silence, Harry sipping his coffee, my muesli dry and tasteless against my tongue. I wanted to ask him questions. Scream in his goddamn face. I wasn't a violent person, but if I'd been my mother, I'd have yanked him out of bed and told him to go for a walk to clear his head. Get outside and mow the lawn. She would have chased me out with the mop, telling me I wasn't getting my pocket money until I'd cleaned my room.

Fortunately for Harry, I wasn't my mother, but something had to give because this wasn't a healthy friendship for anyone, least of all for the two of us in this bed.

We had two weeks to go before Eddie and Joe's wedding, for which I was Joe's best man and Harry here was supposed to stand up for Eddie. I had no doubt for the two of them, the wedding would be everything they had dreamed of. But for Harry, it would be another disaster unless we got some serious intervention underway. For me? I didn't know how, where or when, but my heart felt like it was about to split wide open, and that...

That would be the biggest disaster of all.

chapter three

Harry

"Let's move on to page four. On the thirteenth of October, a payment of three hundred and ten thousand pounds was made to a Chantal Williams. Any thoughts on why this payment was made and who Chantal Williams is in relation to T and L Limited?"

The over-ambitious investigator from His Majesty's Customs and Excise had asked me too many questions already, and it was only Monday. Where work had once been me going into my dad's office and fiddling around with a bit of paperwork and twiddling my thumbs, this... This was not even funny.

"No clue."

I sounded juvenile, but I was out of my depth, and that now familiar unease in my chest was back. It wasn't the first time I'd geared up to have a panic attack in front of these people, but even though they frequently apologised for their intrusive questions and relentless pressure, answering their perfectly reasonable requests didn't get any easier. I suspected this Chantal was probably another of my dad's many so-called lady friends.

He'd never been able to keep his dick in his pants, not even when my mother had been around.

"Let's move on to the fourteenth of October. A withdrawal of ten thousand pounds from Lloyds Bank, cash, made with your father's company card. The same day another failed payment was made to Her Majesty's tax and revenue. This was also the same day the house insurance on Willow Trees House was due, a payment that bounced, meaning that your home was now uninsured. Can I cast your mind back to the claim submitted to Lloyds Insurance two weeks earlier?"

The rustling of paper was making me feel dizzy, and I wished I was anywhere but here—'here' being the soon-to-be former offices of Thunder and Lightning Limited, once Britain's leading supplier of industrial lighting and bespoke electrical solutions, the company that had made my family fortune. My father's pride and joy. I couldn't help snorting out loud, which made the investigator to my left stare at me in disgust. Well, I had nothing more to prove. Nobody left to impress. The remains of what had once been a company with a handsome turnover was now just relentless bankruptcy meetings and an investigation into insurance fraud. On top of the enormous iceberg of shit that my father had left in my capable hands, I was now the CEO of this heap of rusted metal, and as such, it was down to me. I had no answers to give because...

I'd wanted to take control, I'd been groomed for it. I'd always known this company would one day be mine. But when I had tried to push Dad into modernising, expanding into new technology and perhaps even downsizing in the areas where we were clearly not making a profit, he'd dismissed me like an annoying pest and told me to wind my neck in and go learn from the bottom. *Go check those shipping labels and proofread next week's contracts.* I had, but things had come back full circle, over and over again. I should have gone to uni, not let Dad talk me into going straight into work because *look at me now!* I had no education, no qualifications, and apart from the inevitable bankruptcy and bloody tax evasion charges, I had no future. No hope. Fuck.

I stood up in the middle of another question and excused myself, heading for the coffee maker. I needed to get out of here, but I knew I couldn't leave. The questions would keep coming, most of which I wouldn't be able to answer. I'd felt trapped for so long that I'd forgotten how to escape. Not that there would ever be any way out of this with my dignity intact. So I stood there and tried to concentrate on the blinking lights on the machine, showing too many different options for my fried brain to compute. I just wanted espresso, extra strong, preferably now. I stabbed my finger against the display.

"Mr Thunder, did you manage to complete the updated spreadsheet as we requested?"

I may have been an idiot, but I wasn't stupid, and I did know some parts of this company like the back of my hand. I knew the systems we'd used, the people, the stockroom—I'd even bought the Italian espresso machine for the fancy boardroom we were currently occupying. We wouldn't get to keep it; it had already been earmarked for removal by the bailiffs. But I did produce great spreadsheets. I went over and turned my laptop around to display my work—a pristine, easy-to-read, comprehensive breakdown of our current creditors, assets and employee costs.

Employees. Population one. That would be me. Well...and Maggie, who had officially retired but came in to water the pot plants on a Tuesday and push her mop around my desk every Thursday. I could no longer afford to pay her, but she still came, regular as clockwork, with a flask of tea for herself since someone had nicked the old kettle in the staffroom.

My hands shook as I returned to the coffee maker, hoping there were still enough beans in there to reward me with another shot. Even though I'd been raised to one day lead this company, I still didn't have a clue how to deal with people. Not that I could blame my woeful people skills for bankrupting this piece of shit. That part hadn't been my fault, and it was the only thing that kept me going. My father had syphoned off every bloody asset, cheerfully aided by my mother, who had sued him for every penny, helped along by Dad's mate Bernie, who had dipped into the funds like he actually worked here. It hadn't stopped there. Once the word was out of how much trouble the company was in, it had suddenly become a free-for-all. I'd even caught Connor in the storeroom selling off our most valuable spare parts on his private eBay account. I was only twenty-three, and that had been a lot to deal with. No wonder my people skills were lacking.

"Are you all right, Mr Thunder?" That was the other investigator. A middle-aged woman wearing a suit my mother would have frowned at. No doubt it was from a supermarket brand, and the jacket was fraying at the hem. I was not only my father's son; my mother had also taught me a thing or two about dressing to impress. I owned some fine suits, not that I would ever wear them again.

"All good," I mumbled, trying to take a sip of the coffee. My heart was beating faster than was healthy, and the pressure in my chest was once again building. I needed to calm down. I needed to get out of here.

"Have you got anyone at home? Any friends you can rely on?"

Stupid question. She of all people knew I had nothing left. I was on friendlier terms with the local bailiff team than I was with my relatives. And friends? I moved my head in an ambiguous attempt at a nod and tried to smile. Her expression said it all. Pity. Concern. Yeah, my face was still a mangled mess, and the shiner under my eye was impressive in the wrong way, but I wasn't here to impress anyone. To be honest, I'd stopped caring.

I smiled when all I wanted was to cry, especially thinking back to this weekend. That was how pathetic I'd become. Where I'd once lived for socialising and parties, these days I dreamed of hanging out with Owen, sleeping next to him, waking up in the morning to his insanely annoying chit chat and getting a cup of coffee in bed. Warm toast buttered just right. I barely even knew the guy, but he was the only person I felt at ease with, the only one who didn't pester me for All The Truths, though he did ask me all the right questions. I simply chose not to answer them, and he let me. Just patched me up when I lost it, picked me off the ground when I couldn't get up anymore.

I wasn't an alcoholic. I'd grown up with my mother's addictions and my father's constant lies. I knew where the line was drawn, and I couldn't afford to drink these days, but I did so when I could. It was the only thing that, for a little while, made my life fuzzy at the edges. The only time I could forget what a complete crater of a nail bomb my life had become. I lived in constant chaos on the inside, parcelled up in my last remaining clean suit. I couldn't bring myself to ask for help. When I drank, I didn't have to pretend I had my shit together. People knew I was a drunk idiot and let me get on with it. I didn't even have to tell people to look after me, they just did. And I bloody knew how stupid that all sounded, but when you were me, there were very few options left.

"Have you found a place to live?" The woman nattered on. No, I hadn't. I had no income, and my meagre savings were quickly running out. I didn't bother telling her. She knew anyway. She had my entire life down to my last pair of socks, right there on that spreadsheet.

"The bank will foreclose on the Willow Trees House on Saturday, Mr Thunder. Are you sure you will have all your personal effects removed by then?"

Such bullshit, such fake concern. They hadn't had any concern the first time they raided my house for valuables, not that there had been anything left after my mother moved out. The art that had once adorned the walls, those fancy kitchen appliances, my dad's collection of stupid cars, all the little luxuries of my childhood? Long gone. I was lucky I still had a mattress on my bed frame, hot running water and credit on my phone.

Life essentials, they'd said. Well, until Saturday, apparently, when I'd be asked to hand over the keys and remove myself from land that was no longer mine.

I wiped the tear off my cheek and tried to compose myself. What would Owen have said? He made me laugh. *"Babes,"* he would have said. *"Chin up, babes. It's a new day tomorrow."* Then he would probably have tripped on his goddamn carpet and spilled that green tea he drank all over himself. He was such a dork. Oversized and over the top. That was Owen. But he was also the kindest person I knew and gave the best hugs. I could have done with someone like him. Not that I would ever ask for stuff like that. I wasn't like those people. I wasn't a touchy-feely person, and I could look after myself. I didn't need anyone.

Or maybe I did, but this wasn't the time or place to admit that.

chapter four

Owen

Wednesday turned out to be my favourite day of this week, not only because I was working on the post-op ward, gaining me access to a proper lunch hour, but also because I got to have lunch with Joe. Hospital shifts meant that we rarely worked at the same time, but the sun was shining as Joe and I took our coffee and sandwiches down to the small park behind A&E, rolling up our scrub trousers to catch some rays as we sat down.

"Summer..." Joe almost moaned in anticipation. "I can't wait for summer."

"Yet you chose to get married in spring," I teased.

"Wasn't my choice. My mum has gone full-on mad planning this wedding. I mean, Eddie's mum is so chilled about it all, while my mum is having daily panic attacks over seating plans and champagne brands and what kind of glasses to use for the chocolate mousse. I'm a little freaked out, to be honest." He took a bite out of his sandwich and sighed deeply as he chewed.

"You? Freaked out? You just have to turn up and look gorgeous, and Eddie will love you forever. I, on the other hand, have to deliver a speech, which I've already written and already hate, and everyone will laugh at me. Not to mention—"

"That Harry will be expecting to speak too, and that Eddie is already panicking about that not-so-small disaster. What do we do about Harry? I don't want to be mean. Eddie wants him to be his best man, and I can respect that, but it's my wedding too."

"Harry..." I had to take a moment to regroup. "I need to sit down with him. It's a week until the rehearsal dinner, but I don't know where to start."

"Well, it's not like we don't know what's going on. Eddie has a mate in the council planning department. The Thunder and Lightning site has been sold. Demolition starts in three weeks to make way for a discount supermarket. Aldi or Lidl. Can't remember which one."

"I love Lidl." I smiled and then dropped my stupidness. Joe was worried, and rightly so. I was having a small crisis myself, wondering how to deal with it.

"Harry's gone through a lot in the last six months," Joe rambled on. "It's not fair on him, but I don't know how we can help. Eddie's tried. He took him out for lunch last week, and he clammed up as soon as Eddie mentioned work." Joe looked lost in thought, nibbling on his sandwich. "He's Eddie's oldest friend, they went to nursery together, and I like Harry...when he is Harry. I don't particularly like him when he's drinking. He becomes a whole different person, and it kind of swooshes me back to senior school. Harry was a dick at school. He hated my guts and made my life miserable. Just having him around makes me feel really small and stupid again, and I don't like it. I don't want to feel like that."

Joe suddenly looked sad, and I didn't like it. Joe was the happiest person ever, all sunshine and colours and endless smiles. Yet we had both been traumatised by our teenage years. Growing up out and proud, I'd always thought I'd brought it on myself, but these days, I wore my Pride pins with just that. Pride. Neatly pinned on my rainbow work lanyard, with all my colours on show. I didn't take any shit anymore, and neither did Joe, with his own colourful lanyard and collection of rainbow pins adorning his ID.

"I know what you mean." I took a sip of my coffee, warm and milky and soothing to my heart that was once again beating out of control. I had some strange reactions to the mention of Harry's name. All these ridiculous feelings bubbled up to the surface whenever someone said something mean about that man. I wanted to defend him, even though I knew Joe was right. Harry was mean and horrible after two drinks, out of control by drink number three and full-on nasty after four, and there was not much anyone could do to change that. "I keep thinking about what I can do. How I can help him see that there's a problem. I like him, and I really don't want to upset him."

"Of course you do, and that tiny crush on him you're nursing isn't particularly helping the issue, is it?"

I nudged his shoulder making him go, "Oi!" as a drip of coffee spilled from his cup.

"It's just a small crush. I know it will lead nowhere. Harry's straight."

"Oh, you never know. I spent months being told that Eddie was the most heterosexual human being ever to have walked the planet. I was kind of wrong."

"And thank God for that."

"I know. I'm lucky. And Eddie is...I love him. He's amazing."

"And Harry is trouble. On a grand scale." I wanted to add something nice, but there wasn't a word to describe what I was feeling. Worry? Anguish? Unrequited bloody crushes. Again. Always, as it turned out. I'd never had a lasting relationship, mostly because I always fell for the wrong guys. Straight guys, closeted guys, idiots.

"I don't know if Harry is even on the scale of being anything...but..." Joe trailed off.

"You can say it, Joseph," I said in my poshest voice. "Harold will never fancy me. I am barking completely up the wrong tree."

"You are indeed, young Owen. Harold, is..." He stopped and snorted. "Harold is about as unattainable as Harry Styles. Not in your league. And there is a ninety-nine per cent chance that he will never understand the wonders of a good session of quality gay sex."

I grinned. Joe was the funniest guy ever, which is why I absolutely adored him—despite him not letting me share his husband. Not even a little bit.

"The wonders of gay sex, you say? Can I remind you that the last time I had sex with anyone, we were still at uni, and the guy I had sex with never spoke to me again."

"Months of pining and another broken heart. Took a lot of tequila and Netflix to get over that one."

"Yeah." That was me in a nutshell. I always fell hard and fast, and then I nursed a broken heart for months when nothing would come of it, which was why I stayed away from hook-ups these days. More heartbreak than they were worth. "I've tried talking to Harry about his drinking. He's not easy to crack."

"He won't ask for help. He's too stubborn, and all that toxic masculinity that he throws around like a badge of honour—he'll never admit there's something wrong. Not to any of us, anyway."

"You have to ask the right questions," I said gingerly. "And I don't know what those are yet."

"Well, your track record of asking the right questions? Hmm..." Joe laughed. "We know what you tend to ask, and those questions are not the ones people want to answer."

"Just because my lifelong ambition is to find out who tops in your relationship doesn't mean I am a bad human being," I protested. "I bet Eddie likes it. I bet you do too."

"I am a respectable man and I will never tell. You know that. My private life is sacred," Joe said with a pompous twang to his voice. "Incidentally, I know you asked Kim. He'll never tell either."

"He knows?" I squealed, and Joe laughed.

"He knows nothing. Come on, Owen. Privacy is a thing. But then, we all know what you want to do to poor Harry. He'd never see it coming."

"Don't be crude." I huffed, but I still smiled. We did this all the time. Laughing about serious things made them a little lighter, but the fact that Joe was getting all the love and sex and cuddles in the world while I was getting nothing would always be a sore point.

"You know we love you, Owen. You're family, whether you like it or not. I mean, I would never have made it through the whole nursing course without you pushing me and feeding me and mothering me and keeping me from falling apart."

"It wasn't easy," I teased with a smile. We had history, and those years of my life would always count as my happiest.

"Remember the first day at uni? You sat in that corner looking terrified, and I sat in the opposite one ready to faint. And I thought I could see a rainbow pin on your jacket, but you kept wrapping the collar under your neck and chewing your nails, and in the end, I had to come up and ask you what it was."

"And instead of saying, 'Hello, fine young man, is that a rainbow pin on your lapel?'..." Joe was laughing so hard, he could barely speak.

"Yeah, not my finest moment."

"You said, 'Oh...you gay?' No wonder you're single when that's the pickup line you come out with."

"You were shaking almost as much as I was—in my case out of fear that I'd seen wrong and you'd get up and punch me or something. Senior school did quite a number on us both. I was terrified that day. Then you stood up and I thought all my nightmares had come true. First day of uni and I was about to be beaten up by a kid in a parka wearing a rainbow pin."

"I haven't got a violent bone in my body!" Joe smiled. "And we spent that first lecture constantly texting each other. I think you saved my future that day. Had I not met you, I'd have been on the first train home."

"Ditto. I'm super grateful for you, babes. You know that."

"So what do we do about Harry?"

"I don't know." The sandwich suddenly tasted stale in my mouth. "Apart from making up some lie at the wedding about a massive shortage of alcohol in town and forcing everyone to drink water."

"Nah. He's oblivious to the fact that everyone is on to him. He has no income, and knowing what we know about the state of his dad's company and the house being sold, I don't even want to guess what state he'll be in."

I sighed. "Don't worry. I'll call him later and see if he wants to meet up. Just have a chat perhaps."

"A chat is good. Just don't ask him if he's gay."

"Shut up, Joseph."

"You've got crumbs in your stubble, Owen."

"I look good with crumbs in my stubble, thank you very much."

"Anyway, I've gotta go. Need to pee before I go back on duty."

"Fine." I stood up, shook the crumbs off my lap and scratched my stubble just in case.

"Rein that crush in," Joe said quietly. "You deserve better."

"I know," I replied. Then I grinned. "I bet you top."

He stuck his tongue out at me, leaving me standing there, letting the burn in my chest build. Once again, he knew me better than I knew myself. Well, who was I kidding? My nights were spent dreaming of Harry. Of him letting me kiss him. Having him sleep in my arms. Lazy snuggles under the duvet. Soft strokes against my skin.

But that wasn't reality, and my mobile ringing shook me out of my stupid daydreams.

"Yo," I huffed into the phone.

"Hey," Eddie said solemnly. Hmm. OK.

"You all right?" I asked. "What's up?"

"Can you come over after work? I...I think we need to sort Harry out."

chapter five

Harry

I could hear them talking. I'd been wide awake from the moment the doorbell rang and Owen's voice boomed through the walls. Not that Eddie was being any more discreet. If he'd been annoyed with me earlier, he was full-blown fuming now.

"I found him face down on the driveway, Owen. Comatose! He hadn't even locked the front door, and the gates were wide open. We've got a bloody week, more or less, before the wedding, and he's just getting worse. We can't keep doing this!"

The bedroom door wasn't closed, so I heard every word. They weren't even attempting to keep their voices down, talking about me like I wasn't there. I didn't remember being dragged up the stairs, but I was painfully aware that I was splayed out, fully clothed, on top of Joe and Eddie's unmade double bed. They should have bought a king-size. Or super-king-size like Owen's bed. At least the both of us could fit in there with plenty of room to spare. Here, in this bed, I couldn't even imagine Joe or Eddie fitting in it. The two of them probably slept all spooned up like the joined-at-the-hips idiots they were.

Even thinking about it made the anxiety in my chest flutter back to life. I was pushing every boundary here, and I knew it. I hadn't meant to get drunk in the middle of the day, but I'd been clearing out what had once been my parents' walk-in closet, dumping my father's stupid clothes into a charity collection bag, and I'd come across a box containing what must have been a gift. An extravagant one too. God only knew who'd bought my dad a litre bottle of aged Scotch whisky in a fancy velvet box, but I'd opened it and drunk it. Most of it. Not quite enough to kill me, but I hadn't thought about it like that while I was gulping it straight from the bottle. The alcohol had burned nicely, slipping down my throat, and I had welcomed the haze it brought to my head so my mind wasn't whizzing in a constant state of half panic.

I had a whole house to empty before Saturday. I had nowhere to live and a sum total of £253 pounds on a cash card to live off, which meant a hotel was out of the question and an Airbnb would last me less than a week.

I honestly had no idea what to do, and the stress of my whole life disappearing into the skip on the driveway was crippling me. I couldn't even pay for the skip, but that was the last of my worries right now.

My belongings—I'd dumped it all. I had a bag of clothes by the front door, my passport and a few trinkets from my childhood that I still wasn't strong enough to part with in a small box. A few faded photographs. I didn't know why I'd kept them, maybe because of the smiling kid standing on the lawn with his parents? I didn't even know who any of those people were anymore.

I'd tried to ring my mother, and my call had once again gone to her Spanish voicemail. Not that I could afford a ticket to Tenerife. I could barely afford to eat.

"What has he taken?" I heard Owen's feet thunder up the stairs and didn't even flinch when the light came on and he threw himself down on his knees next to the bed. And there it was. He was taking my pulse and staring into my eyes like I was about to pass away.

I wasn't. I wasn't even hungover. Apart from a little dizzy spell as he yanked me up to a sitting position on the bed, I was fine.

"What did you take?" he demanded, his voice low and stern. "What exactly did you take, Harry?"

"Chill!"

"Your pulse is far too high, and I don't like the look of you right now."

"I don't like the look of you either," Eddie said, crowding in behind him. "Harry, you fucking dick."

"I didn't take nothing!" I hissed out, finally following their train of thought. "Jesus, no. I'm not trying to top myself if that's what you're thinking. No. No, hell, no."

"Then what are you doing?" Owen pleaded in that voice that was starting to grate on me. Constant disappointment. Always ending up like this.

"It's not like I have anything else to keep me out of trouble. I found a bottle of thirty-year-old Ardbeg. It was either throw it in the skip or drink the damn thing. OK?"

"That's enough to kill you if you're not careful," Owen pointed out.

"Harry..." Eddie was losing it, and he knew it. He walked out the door, letting it slam shut behind him. Yeah. I could relate. I would've slammed the door on me too. Owen followed right behind him, the door bouncing back against the wall as he left.

I knew what I was doing, but I couldn't think straight. It had given me respite from everything else, just for an hour or two or whatever. To be honest, I had no idea what time it was, and I curled up on the bed again as the familiar nausea hit. I hadn't eaten a thing today. Not by choice. I was trying to save every penny for next week. Until I had a plan. Fuck. I had no plan, and Owen was right. My heart was beating far too fast, and now he was out in the hallway shouting at Eddie, and Eddie was shouting back, and I kind of hoped Joe would come back before the two of them got into a fight.

"I'm taking him home." That was Owen. I was officially a pity case.

"No. We're driving him home and dumping him at the gates, next to the rest of that whisky."

"While I agree we should let him hit rock bottom, this is not the time or place."

Owen. Bless his little heart. Rock bottom, my arse. How much further could I go?

"Owen." Eddie again. Pleading. "Look. Don't do this to yourself."

"I have no bloody choice, do I?" Yeah, Owen was mad. And I tried to sit myself up so I could get out there and tell those two idiots that I could walk myself home fine and finish off that whiskey so I could get out of their hair for good. I felt like an argument myself, but I didn't even have the strength to get off the bed, my head spinning like crazy as I tried to throw my legs over the side.

I couldn't stay here. Eddie and Joe only had one bedroom, and their sofa was not an option. I didn't want to wake up here and get all the aggro from Joe in the morning. He didn't like me, at all. He tolerated my presence in small doses, but I wasn't his favourite person and never would be. I didn't blame him because, yeah, I'd spent most of my teens being a total twat, and as it turned out, I was still an attention-seeking imbecile and a certified dumbass. A better human would have figured this out a long time ago and sorted my dad out and fixed things and wound down the spending and fucking sold the house if I'd had to. Anything but the mess I was in now. If I'd spiralled before, I was now at the very bottom of the earth, crawling around in the dirt looking for any scrap of decency.

I had to smile because that part was a lie. There was nothing decent left about me. I lied and drank and made messes that I struggled to clear up.

"You have bigger problems than Harry Thunder." Eddie's voice came through. "You have work and your mum and a whole life, and the last thing you need is having Harry camp out in your bed. I mean, think of yourself. It will drive you insane."

"Now you sound like Joe."

"And Joe's right. You need to get over this stupid crush on him and move on. Having him live with you? Come on, Owen. Don't do this to yourself."

"I don't have a crush on Harry."

Yeah, he did. Even I knew that. Had I milked it? Fuck, yes. Was I a piece of shit? Absolutely.

"Well, you didn't mind when Harry was all over you at school. Yeah, Mr High-and-Mighty!"

Owen could be mean when he wanted, and now Eddie was gasping for breath, no doubt ready to deliver a comeback.

"Harry never crushed on me. Don't be ridiculous."

I could picture the eyeroll Owen was delivering, and it made me grin. Just for a second. My face still hurt when I smiled.

"Well, why else is he still around? He idolises you something stupid and follows you around like a bad smell."

"And he sleeps in your bed. I don't think I'm the one with a Harry problem."

Oh. Low blow.

"Harry doesn't even like me. He's only in my bed because I'm the one who has to drag your mate home when he's drunk enough to piss himself."

"Owen, shut the fuck up."

Eddie didn't swear, but I could feel it vibrating in the air. He was stressed, and to an unhealthy level. I recognised it well because I was sitting up and *Shut the fuck up!* was right there on the tip of my tongue.

Somehow, I managed to get my stupid body out into the hallway and looked down to see Eddie and Owen standing on the stairs staring up at me.

"I'll leave." I didn't know what else to say. "I know when I'm not wanted. And don't worry about the wedding. I won't be there." The words tumbled out of my mouth as I sank to my knees. I was tired. So tired and drained. "And so what if you were my bloody hero at school?" My mouth was on a roll, and I couldn't make it stop. "I mean, we all wanted to be as cool as Eddie Sumner. The girls were falling at your feet, and the boys thought you were brilliant. It didn't matter what I did. Everyone always liked you better. I just wanted to be you. Not me. I mean? It was..."

I had to stop and breathe. In. Out. My vision blacked out a little as I knelt there on the floor. Pathetic. How low could I go?

Lower, as it turned out, because next thing I knew I was on the floor and had Owen talking gibberish at me. Something about blood sugar and did Joe have a blood-pressure machine? Apparently, he owned both because he was a bloody nerd, and the next thing, I was being manhandled around on the floor and...

"Ouch!"

"Shut up, Harry." Owen was still mad at me. Good. He'd stuck something in my finger and was trying to squeeze blood out of me. Not only gay but also a vampire of some kind.

"Stop squirming. I need to check your blood sugar. Seriously? When did you last eat? I bet like never. Fuck you."

"Fuck you right back."

Yes, that was the level we were at, and it made me want to cry. I was spilling out far too many truths here and the embarrassment in my head wasn't even measurable. Rock bottom? Yeah. I was there, all right.

"Why the hell would you want to be me?" Eddie whined, now sitting on the floor next to me. "My mum bought my school uniform second hand so she could save up for my school trips. I spent most of my teens being too bloody confused about everything. You? You had all the money and all the friends, and yeah, you were a right dick. There. I said it."

"You've said it before," I managed to pant out. "No need to apologise. I know I was a dick. I still am. I do have some self-awareness, you know."

"So, why the hell are we here, Harry?" Eddie shouted, dropping his head into his hands and grunting in frustration. I wanted to grunt too.

"Because things suck?" I couldn't even think of a better way to describe it.

"Things *don't* suck."

I could see Eddie clearly now, as Owen had propped me up and was forcing a glass of orange juice down my throat.

"That may come back up," I warned.

"It better not! I'm taking you down to A&E."

"Don't."

I was suddenly more terrified of that option than the prospect of having to face Joe coming home and finding me on his hallway carpet.

"I drank a load of whisky. Stupid move, I agree. I haven't eaten anything...I mean. Can't..." It was hard to say the words. "Afford it."

They didn't say anything back. Just stared at me. Not in shock, I didn't think, but for a minute I couldn't read them. Either of them.

"Thank you for finally telling the truth," Eddie said, and he seemed calmer.

"You need to eat," Owen said again.

"Yes, Mother."

"I really don't like you right now," Eddie muttered.

"I know, and that's what you always say. I do stupid shit, and you tell me you don't like me."

"It's something you and I need to work on. But this drinking has to stop. And I think we all deserve some truths out of that mouth of yours for once, Harry. Stop the bullshit."

"OK." I laughed. It hurt. And it wasn't funny. "But I didn't have a crush on you."

Eddie Sumner, bloody golden gym-bunny boy and idiot of the century, the guy I had known since we toddled around my mum's paddling pool, smiled at me, and it wasn't a kind smile.

His mum had once known my mum.

She'd had friends back then, before the paddling pool was replaced with a proper swimming pool and she'd left those friends behind and made friends with her bottles of gin instead. I didn't blame her. I was doing the exact same thing myself.

"I don't have anything left." I admitted. It hurt to admit it, but I had to. I had no more lies to give. Now more fucks either, it seemed, as Owen wrapped his arms around me.

He never hugged me when I was sober. Now he did.

"I'm not gay," came out of my stupid mouth.

"Of course you're not," he whispered into my neck.

Eddie rolled his eyes and said nothing, but I could see the words forming on his lips. *"Shut the fuck up, Harry."*

chapter six

Owen

He'd been on his best behaviour since Wednesday. Quiet but civil. He'd wash and get dressed, then sit on the sofa, silently eating every scrap of food I put in front of him.

There had been accusations of trust issues when I'd laid down my demands and forced him to add me on his phone so I could track him and see where he was at all times. I wasn't going to fish him out of the gutter and was frank in telling him that I still suspected he had some kind of messed-up death wish. But he'd just nodded as I'd issued ultimatums and threats. Yes, he agreed he needed a job, and no, he would not touch a drop of alcohol, and yes, he understood there would be rent due and he had no rights to change any of these demands until he could prove himself sensible and sober.

I was still salty and he knew it, but in his defence, he went to his house and finished up doing whatever he'd been doing there without any further incidents. He said he'd even put the empty whisky bottle in the recycling bin, like a good citizen of earth. I'd laughed at that, but the silent treatment had continued, and I'd come home from work to find him curled up on the sofa. The bruising around his face had faded to a quaint yellow, which only made the dark circles under his eyes look worse.

There was a bin liner of stuff at the end of the bed and a small box at the bottom of the stairs with his name on it. He'd moved in then.

Truthfully, that was the only thing that kept me going. I tried to talk to him, but he recoiled from any attempt at a productive conversation, and at night, he slept on the very edge of the bed, as far away from me as possible. I got it, I did. He was embarrassed and broken, and I was a little too much in his face. It wasn't a comfortable situation, and we both knew it.

Now it was Saturday morning, and I was perched on the sofa with Eddie and Joe sitting opposite, all of us nursing cups of tea.

"We need a plan," Eddie started.

"He'll be up in a sec," I replied. I didn't like talking behind his back. He was part of this team and needed to know that.

"Has he?" Joe said quietly. "Stayed sober?"

"I have no alcohol in the house," I assured him. "I'm not stupid. He's eating and sleeping. That's the good part. His mental health? I have no idea where he's at in his head."

"Talking about me again?" Here he was. Wrapped in the duvet with his hair on end. I wanted so badly to get him a haircut, make him feel smart and professional again. He'd always been clean cut, in ironed collared tops and smooth suits. Bed-head Harry dressed in my duvet, though?

"Good morning," Eddie said cheerily. "Yes, we're talking about you. And if you sit down and behave, I might even go make you a coffee."

"Dickhead," Harry muttered.

"Suit yourself," Eddie retaliated, crossing his arms. "Just be nice. For once."

"It's Saturday, and the bank is foreclosing on my house in two hours. I think I'm allowed to be a little bit...un-nice today."

Nobody looked sympathetic, including me.

"I'll drive you there later to pick up the rest of your stuff," Eddie offered.

"Thanks," came from the duvet. "But I'll go on my own. I'd rather not have an audience to officially becoming homeless."

"You're not homeless. You're renting space in my fine abode right here, babes."

"I'm squatting on the right side of your bed, *babes*. I don't even have wardrobe space."

Joe snorted, which was good. It made Eddie smile, and we needed to kill the tension in the room.

"How bad is it?" Joe questioned, putting his cup of tea down.

"It's now down to a full personal bankruptcy. Next hearing with the insolvency service is in two weeks, and since my dad mortgaged the house against the company—fuck knows what he was thinking—as the company is bankrupt and I can't even pay his backdated golf membership, creditors are clawing everything back. At least with declaring myself bankrupt, that should stop. That's what my adjudicator is proposing."

"Your...what?" I had to ask. I had no clue about these things, but Harry was surprisingly sharp.

"Adjudicator. The guy who decides if I've fucked up enough to ruin my chances of ever clearing my debts. Well, not my debts. I inherited them when the house became mine. Dad even put my name on the utilities, his car loans and the goddamn pool-cleaning service. I'm being sued by the gardener and..." He had to stop and take a breath. "I'm not looking for sympathy here, things are just the way they are. It's been a little overwhelming, but the end result should hopefully be manageable. There will be restrictions on my life for the next couple of years. I can't borrow money, run a company or get involved in any kind of business venture. I can work, though, but it's not like anyone in my field would employ the guy who broke Thunder and Lightning, sold off its assets and went bankrupt in the process."

"At least you tried," Joe said, looking a little lost.

"Too little, too late." Harry sighed. "Had I known—I mean, had my dad told me how much debt he was in—then I could have at least stood a chance."

"Your dad was a dick," Eddie said, always eloquent.

"He's not here to defend himself," Joe pointed out, naturally.

"Nah." Harry shook his head. "You're right. He was a dick. Did you know that I am not an only child? Bastard didn't have the guts to tell me, but the child maintenance meeting I had to sit through was rather enlightening."

"Oh, babes," I said. He looked kind of broken.

"I've got at least five younger siblings by three different women. Not that it matters. Nothing I can do about that either. It would have been nice to know, but I can't change that. I very much doubt any of those kids want the bankrupt loser son of their deadbeat dad turning up on their lawn hoping for a meaningful relationship."

"You're probably right," Eddie said, twisting his hands.

"I know I'm right. If someone had turned up on my lawn, I would've punched them in the face."

"Things are a bit raw now, babes, but in the future...you never know."

Harry snorted and changed the subject. "So, rehearsal dinner tonight."

"Five o'clock," Joe confirmed.

"Am I still invited?" He looked a little scared, and I didn't blame him.

"My mum will have kittens if she has to change the seating plan again."

"Your mum will have a heart attack if *anything* changes now. Jane has been taking this wedding planning a little too seriously."

"Mum is nuts." Joe sighed. "But yes. You're coming. And there will be rules."

"No drinking," Harry muttered.

"We'll all take turns hanging out with you. Keeping you in line," I said sternly.

"So don't even think about having a drink," Joe threatened. I was impressed.

"Wasn't. Just don't...like, mention this. I want to fly under the radar rather than being the guy in the corner everyone's throwing a pity party for. It's your wedding."

"Thank you," Joe said, sipping his tea. "It's just going to be a few people having a nice, quiet, family dinner. No stress."

"What's the rehearsal about then?" I had to ask, and Eddie rolled his eyes.

"Some kind of American thing Jane read about. It's a bloody dinner party. End of."

"I told you," Joe said. "My mum is nuts."

"We're *all* nuts," I muttered. "Why the hell couldn't you just elope to Vegas or the Maldives or something?"

Harry smiled at that. The mood was much nicer when he smiled.

"Yes, Edward. Why aren't you in the Maldives?" he asked.

"Because Joe's mum would kill us. And Joe's dad hates flying and...yeah. I don't know. I just want to marry Joe and get on with life."

"Honeymoon." I swooned. "Where are you going again?"

"Southampton." Joe grinned as Eddie swiftly averted being tackled on the sofa. "Because my lovely husband-to-be forgot to put in for leave, and I get to have two weeks at home and a weekend in Southampton."

"It's a five-star hotel! One Michelin star!" Eddie tried to defend himself. "Beach views!"

"Beach views... It's April, Eddie. Not a chance of even dipping our toes in the water." Joe pretended to sulk, although he'd been majorly pissed off when they'd had to cancel their dream honeymoon and reschedule it for November. It wasn't what they'd planned, but Joe still leaned in and kissed his fiancé, and apparently, I was doing that face. The one that made Harry box my shoulder.

"Stop drooling."

"Can't help it."

"Owen!" Joe warned. I laughed.

They left in a flurry of laughter and kisses and hugs, the air feeling a little bit lighter as I plonked myself back on the sofa.

"You want another coffee?" I offered, but Harry wrapped the duvet tighter around himself and shook his head.

"Why do you always kiss them on the lips?" he asked. Trust him to be frank and direct.

"You mean, Eddie and Joe? We're mates, and we always hug and kiss when we meet."

"And you hug and snog when you say goodbye. On the lips."

"So? Nothing wrong with that."

"You never hug me. Or snog me for that matter. I'm starting to think this crush is just for show." He was trying to rile me up again, perhaps even make me laugh, but I was having none of it.

"You're not that kind of person. You're all ice and venom, and whenever I come anywhere near you, it's all prickles and thorns. It's not like you invite affection, Harry, and people pick up on that."

"I'm not all ice and whatever," he muttered.

"And I don't have a crush on you."

"Ha! You do. Even Eddie says so."

I had to smile, because when Harry was in a good mood? Cute.

"I think you're very attractive, and yes, you are totally my type. But I have morals and standards, Harry. I would never do anything uninvited and unconsented, and that includes touching you and snogging you. Are we clear? If you want a hug, just ask. Those are always available."

"You sound like it's all part of the service. Clean bed, coffee and food. Hugs on request."

"Well, it's something like that."

"So, why don't you hug and kiss me?" His face was suddenly an open book, and I could only laugh because he was, once again, being ridiculous.

"You, babes, would punch my face in if I did. So don't even go there."

The phrase was supposed to make him smile. But he wasn't smiling. If anything, he looked confused.

"I'm going to go get my stuff. Drop off the keys to the house and forget I ever had a home."

"OK, babes," I replied, watching him shuffle away with the duvet around his waist. There was still a faint bruise on his back.

I wasn't falling for any of his attention-seeking bullshit, but at least he was talking, agreeing to things, following the rules—I could hear him rumbling around in the bathroom. I'd even washed his trousers like the fool I was, but I'd wanted to reward him for picking up his clothes, which meant he was no longer lounging around the house wearing my oversized T-shirts.

I wasn't going to admit how much I liked seeing him in those T-shirts with his skinny, fluffy legs poking out wearing my socks.

"You're staring out the window again. Daydreaming, are we?"

"Yes, dreaming of you, babes. You know it." I smiled back.

"I knew it. You do love me."

"Of course I do. And next thing you know, I'll be down on one knee asking you to marry me. It'll be super romantic, babes."

I was kidding, and he actually giggled, leaning down to tie up his shoelaces.

"On a serious note, you sure you don't want me to come with you? Pick up your stuff and help you carry? Emotional support?"

"Nah. You're good. But hey, Owen?"

"Yeah?"

He was smiling. And my stomach was going all warm.

"I'm still worried about this crush. You don't even get up to hug me goodbye. I might get run over by a truck walking up the hill, and you'll never see me again."

"Or you might break your neck stepping out the door. Just get out, Harry." I said it in kindness, and he laughed as the door slammed shut behind him.

I was starting to wonder if Eddie was right. Maybe offering to let Harry stay here had been a massive mistake. At the same time, I dreaded him coming back and telling me he'd found a job and a place to rent. Then this small life of imaginary bliss would be over, and Owen Cartwright would once again be single and alone.

Bliss. Who was I kidding? I was living with a straight guy who couldn't even spell friendship. The chance of him even knowing what infatuation meant was close to zero, and there was no way I would ever kiss him. Ever. Nope. Wasn't happening.

chapter seven

Harry

I didn't know what to do with myself. It almost felt like someone had stabbed me with a long, sharp needle and made all the air inside of me escape. Some kind of long, drawn-out whistle where I was suddenly saying far too much and sharing information that I had no business sharing.

Dad had always been big on silences. Keeping secrets. What was said between our walls stayed between those walls—apart from if people were dicks then we were supposed to call them out on it, burn their reputations into submissions. Show them who was boss. Get them back in line. *"Don't let people walk all over you with all that woke shite,"* my dad would say. *"We want results and profit, not any of that emotional bullshit."*

The older I'd got and the more time I'd spent in his shadow, the more I'd started to see through the cracks. My dad had not been a nice bloke. He'd been a man who was so obsessed with money and status that he treated people like garbage. His employees never stayed long, and I'd barely remembered the names of the temps who came in to do our admin before they'd disappeared and been replaced with more. Disposable. Even Maggie, the cleaning lady. He'd barely ever remembered her name, yet she'd brought me a card for my birthday. I'd been embarrassed as anything that day, especially since my dad had just shrugged and said something about birthdays being for children and could I hurry up with the sales report?

Long gone were the huge expensive birthday parties Mum and him used to throw for me, obviously all for show. The last few years he'd been cold and indifferent, flying off the handle as soon as anything didn't go his way. And Mum...I couldn't remember the last time she'd contacted me.

I understood things better now, the enormous pressure Dad had been under, the guilt and the insane mind games he'd played on me. I was no more family than those random women who'd warmed his bed. Yes, I'd known, and I'd pretended not to because that was the way things rolled in our house. No wonder Mum had buggered off, apparently with her solicitor in tow. I knew nothing about that part, but I was beyond caring now.

I'd been disposable too. He could have easily put me through university, let me go have an education and build a life. He hadn't, and I resented everything about that summer, the one when he'd made me withdraw my application and come work for him. I'd slowly figured it out: he'd already been in the red financially, and my uni fees would have been an unwelcome extra expense.

I'd been a spoiled child back then, and I didn't feel any more grown up now, hiding in a wicker chair in the corner of a fancy country hotel restaurant. Everyone was enjoying cocktails in the conservatory, Joe's aunties dressed up in snazzy dresses and Eddie looking uncomfortable and hot in a bow tie. I'd told him he looked like a stiff, and he'd ripped it off, only for Joe's mum to put it back on him. She was stressed, and Joe looked like he wanted to skulk off and hide. I was lucky. I *could* skulk off and hide, so I had, and I was very comfortable in my chair with a bottle of water in my hand, thank you very much.

"Harry! Harry, darling, Jane wants you to come meet...some kind of relative. Who knows? I've lost count already. Are you all right? Sitting here on your own?"

I swallowed slowly to buy some time. I liked Eddie's mum, but I really could do without meeting more relatives and shaking hands and feeling like a right idiot in a suit with a stain down the side of the jacket. I hadn't even ironed it, having thrown all my suits in a bin liner and only dug them out last night, hoping they were half decent. The fact was, they could all have done with a dry clean, and most of them were in a state. Owen had let me hang them up in his wardrobe. They'd looked funny hanging there, mine all crumpled and narrowed shouldered against Owen's well-pressed, huge jackets.

"I'm fine here, Carol. Honestly," I tried as she tutted slightly.

"Jane is...very persistent."

"I know." I smiled. See? Here I was again. Telling truths and actually thinking before I spoke. "It makes me feel really nervous. Too many people. I just need a few minutes."

I didn't need minutes. I needed hours. Years. A new life. A career. I'd settle for a month's minimum wage so I could find a place to live. Feel like a fully-fledged adult again.

I really liked Eddie's mum. Especially when she nodded and went back to the crowded conservatory with the champagne cocktails and stupid little snacks, squeezing Owen's arm as she passed him.

Owen. He looked good in a suit, all cleaned up with his hair done and his beard neatly trimmed, standing in there smiling and making conversation like he owned the place. And my head went into that strange new space, one I had started to recognise. It scared me, because it was a strangely comfortable space. One where I smiled and sunk further into the chair.

I was smiling because somehow he made me...smile. And I was hiding because I had nothing to say, nothing to show for my twenty-three years of life. I wasn't even truthful with myself. I didn't want a place to live because the thought terrified me. I'd been snowed under with all the responsibility that had drowned me over the last year, and I was just starting to come up for air, waking up in the morning with less of the weight of an elephant sitting on my chest. The more of that weight that shifted, the lighter my life was becoming, and the feeling of being so utterly alone in all this had started to clear. That wasn't down to any solicitors or adjudicators or helpful investigators from His Majesty's Customs and Excise. No. I'd had Owen, and even thinking that was terrifying because there was no way that his offer of letting me stay was a permanent one. It had been a usual olive branch of kindness. A few days until I sorted myself out.

I wasn't anywhere near ready to start sorting myself out. Not in that way.

A gust of air pulled me out of my navel gazing as a vision of hot-pink chiffon swirled through the room.

"Harry Thunder!"

Oh...fuck.

"Amelie!"

I stood up as she air-kissed the hell out of me, pinching my arms with her razor-sharp nails.

"OMG, you look like you've been in a car crash! We need to catch up, how long has it been? Years! I bet you're some super-successful businessman now. Was that your car out front? The sportscar? I never know the brands. There are so many of them up in London! I live in London now, did I tell you? Do you follow me on Instagram? Harry?"

I was looking for an escape route, but there was none to be found. Amelie and I had known each other all our lives too, and she'd always been like this. Too many words and not enough fucks given, which was what I'd kind of liked about her, but right now, she was too much of everything.

"I have an apartment in Notting Hill, it's very posh. Far too expensive, but I'm worth it, you know? The whole street below is lined with bars and little cafés. It's just like in those films we used to watch. Living the dream, that's me!"

"Ehhr..." I didn't know what to say. What was there to say? *Me too?* Living the dream? I smiled because everything had somehow become so absurd.

"I'm not coming to the wedding, as I'll be away on a work trip. Busy, me! But Eddie said I could come tonight and at least give them their wedding gift. I had them made especially, matching cufflinks! So cute! I'll expect pictures of them wearing them on their honeymoon!"

"I think they'll probably be mostly naked on their honeymoon." I stuck in there, feeling my stupidness reach new highs. The fuck was wrong with me? "It's really nice to see you, Amelie."

"Remember at school? Oh God, I had such a crush on Eddie! Thought he was the love of my life. Had a bit of a crush on you too at one point, but then I thought, OMG. I'd be Amelie Thunder. Sounds like a soap brand or some kind of dodgy actress! Oh God, where are my manners? So, what do you do for a living now, Harry?"

Wrong question. The one with no answers.

"You all right, babes?"

Thank you, lord above or whatever. Owen appeared from nowhere, and I grasped at his arm like I was drowning.

"Owen, this is Amelie. Went to school with us. Amelie, this is Owen."

"Ooooh!" There it was. Amelie's brain cells working overtime trying to figure it out. I bet she knew Owen too. Amelie had always known everyone. Owen gently squeezed my arm. I liked that he did. That he had my back. God knew, I needed it today.

"So, correct me if I am wrong, but are the two of you together? So exciting! Harry! I'm thrilled! I never knew, but it all makes sense now. You know how you always hung around with Eddie and Joe."

I hadn't always hung around with Eddie and Joe. We'd gone to the same school. I wanted to stop her ramblings right there and figure out a smart comeback to cut her down with, but I'd somehow lost my edge, and this deflated version of me had no idea what to say.

"We live together," Owen said. *Not helping, dude.*

"So cute!" she gushed. "What do you do, Owen?"

"I'm a nurse. Work down at Medway with Joe."

"I do love a man in scrubs." She squealed, squeezing my arm. "Oh, we have good taste in men, Harry. I'm so excited now! It's rainbow central down here—it's so fun to be back home! I never would have guessed! Wow. I'm so happy for you!"

"What do you do then, Amelie?" I deflected, my voice sounding squeaky and weird.

"I'm in production at Netflix. Work on sets, booking staff, and locations. Not as glamorous as it sounds, but I get to rub shoulders with all the celebs, you know! I love it. I'm on the new *White Noise* set next week, so I can't make the actual wedding, but you know? It's all good. I'm just so happy to be here!"

"Amelie..." I said, but she was already gone in a flutter of perfume and pink, having spotted Eddie in the doorway.

"Oh God, babes," Owen whispered. "What was that all about?"

I sighed. "She now thinks we're a couple."

"Of course she does." He laughed. "Well, that will keep her busy for a bit then. Joe will have a fit when she tries to pull that one on him."

"It's..." What the hell was I doing? "I don't mind."

"It's fine, babes. Just laugh it off," he said, staring at me like I had two heads.

"No. I mean, it takes the pressure off, and..." I winked. Like an idiot. "We look cute together. Amelie said so."

"And Amelie would know, would she? Since she works for Netflix or something?" He grinned. "She's funny. I like her."

"She's not subtle, in any way. But she means well. I haven't seen her in years."

"Was she one of your many girlfriends?"

Wrong question, Owen. Wrong fucking question.

chapter eight

Owen

"The look on Eddie's face was priceless!" Harry snorted with laughter and almost tripped over his own feet. We were walking home, down a residential street in the middle of the night. It wasn't far, and we were both stone cold sober, but I also didn't want to ruin the mood by ordering an Uber and forcing the evening to end because once we got home, it would. We would go to bed and Harry would curl up on his edge while I would lie awake on mine. The truth was, I was giddy and happy, and Harry was laughing. This evening had been fun.

"Joe trying to explain 'verse' to his mum was the most cringeworthy thing I've ever seen."

"Yeah, well, he could have just laughed it off."

"And I really like Amelie. She made everything worth it this evening."

He nodded. "She has no shame, does she?"

"She's brilliant."

I'd come across her on the terrace after dinner, casually sipping her champagne with a smile on her face. She'd been much calmer, a world away from the overconfidence she'd displayed earlier in the evening, and the terrace was quiet and deserted, overlooking nothing but darkness.

"Hello, Harry Thunder's boyfriend." She'd grinned, clinking her glass against mine. I'd stuck to water. Needed my head screwed on right.

"We're not really boyfriends," I'd admitted. "Not that I wouldn't."

She got that one, giving me a little giggle.

"I saw how you looked at him. You absolutely would. And I don't blame you. I would too. All-grown-up Harry Thunder turned out to be hot. Who would have thought?"

"Wasn't he hot in school? I bet all the girls were after him."

"Nah. Well…Harry had money, so everyone wanted a piece of that, but Harry was also a bit of a dick. A massive bully, always running his mouth off and getting into trouble. I see he still is. I work in the film industry, and that shiner is the real thing. Makes me a bit sad—I was hoping for better."

"He'll be fine. He's not had it easy." I hadn't wanted to divulge more. It wasn't my place to do so.

"When we were at school, we used to hang out on this old bench in the mornings. Harry was always early and sat there on his own. I mean, we're talking *an hour* before school. He sometimes sat there doing his homework, sometimes just doing nothing. It sounds stupid now, but I was always early too, and I started going in even earlier, so I could sit there with Harry. He was a completely different person when he was on his own, away from all the people he pretended he wanted to impress. We had some brilliant conversations there, about our future, our hopes…dreams. I always wanted to work in film, you know. Build the fantasy into reality. Meet some big superstar and move to Hollywood. My best bet now is pulling one of the crowd extras, someone who'll treat me to a free latte from the catering van. It's not all it seems, the entertainment industry. It's fucking hard work and lonely."

"Welcome to the singles' club then," I'd said with a smile. She'd smiled too and offered me a high-five.

"What were Harry's hopes and dreams then?" I shouldn't have asked, but it was too tempting to ignore.

"Fishing for ammunition, are we, Harry's boyfriend? Or boyfriend-to-be? You have something good going on there. You should go for it."

"Or not. He's a good friend."

I'd been a little economical with the truth there. Some days, Harry made me happy, lying in my bed mocking me for my obsession with white sheets and my cheap instant coffee. Other days, he was a bloke squatting in my flat who gave me nothing in return. Not even rent. It was mean even thinking that, but... Truths. They were right there, always stabbing me in the feels, reminding me I was a giant fool.

"Harry wanted love," she'd said. "He's a real softy at heart. He wanted to be swept off his feet and have someone who would always have his back. He was lonely, always so bloody alone. There could be a hundred people at his party, but he would be all alone in the middle, looking like he wanted to punch a wall."

"Sounds like Harry." He hadn't changed at all. Add alcohol and his wall punching had risen to new heights.

"So what are you going to do about it?" she'd asked with a wink. "I mean. Stupid not to. You're a nice bloke, and...yeah." She'd laughed. "You look cute together. Not that it matters. Happiness matters, and both of you look happy when you're together. Even earlier at dinner, the two of you sat there gossiping like two little grannies."

"Harry's not interested in me that way. I'm a big lump of a man and...not quite his type." I'd tried to be diplomatic so she'd drop the subject, but she'd just sighed and kept going.

"I may not be a neuroscientist or have a degree from the university of hook-ups, but I do see things." She'd put her champagne glass on the banister and turned around to smooth down the front of my shirt. Perhaps a little too intimate, but she'd had her fair share of bubbles, and I'd sensed she was about to say something that would hurt my heart.

"Attraction comes in a million different shades. We're not all hotwired to fall for the pretty boys and the hot girls. Love doesn't work like that, and trust me, I know. I tried it. I met someone at work, one of those mediocre-looking guys, receding hairline, wanted to go to Turkey to get a hair transplant, never seen the inside of a gym, not attractive at all. I tried, but no. I wasn't interested. But he made me laugh—you've never seen anything like it. We used to sit together at lunch, and he would make my day a little brighter. Seriously nice guy. He would have taken me home with him and loved me forever. That's what he used to say. Then we wrapped and all went our separate ways."

"Sounds like you liked him," I'd said.

She'd rolled her eyes. "He texted me a week later and asked me out. I apologised. I mean, I'm not a total bitch, but he wasn't my type."

"Sad. Story of my life." I'd rolled mine too, which made her giggle.

"I've regretted it ever since. Because you see? Stupid. He was lovely. A really kind, genuine man, and he thought I was funny. He laughed at my jokes. Pegged me down when I went off on one of my stupid rants. Calmed me when I was ready to explode. And he liked me, you know? I blew all that because he didn't look like Idris Elba."

"Idris Elba is a little bit old for me, but I like the grey beard he has going on. Very distinguished."

"I *love* an older man! A little bit of life experience and a well-stocked wallet."

"Now you're being silly, Amelie," I'd pretend-scolded her.

"I know. I want what we all want. To find someone who'll give me a hug when I need it and tell me life will be OK. Weddings are the worst. I mean! Look at Eddie and Joe. Sickening. They still look at each other like they want to drag the other into the nearest broom cupboard and shag like rabbits. And they've been together, years. Years!"

"Awful, I agree."

"Us singletons just have to sit here and drink champagne and order another cocktail dress for another wedding and get on with it. Always the guest, never the bride."

"One day, you will be the most stunning bride," I'd told her, and I really meant it.

"Yeah. I can always dream. Sometimes I think it's just that. A pipe dream that will never happen. I talk too much, I'm shallow and stupid and loud and brash and...pink isn't my colour. I love it, though, this dress. But look at everyone else. Subtle, muted colours, and did you see that jumpsuit? It's like wearing pyjamas! To a wedding!"

"Well, it's a dinner party, really."

"Rehearsal dinner. Joe's mum told me. It's *very important*." I loved her sarcasm.

"Very." I spoke fluent sarcasm too.

"Seriously, though, give Harry his happy-ever-after. He deserves it." She'd picked her glass back up and downed the last of her champagne, then slammed the glass down on the bannister, from where it tumbled in silence, falling down into the greenery below. "Oops!"

I'd swallowed a giggle. "They'll find it tomorrow."

"I need to go home to my mum's before I get too drunk. She treats me like I'm still fifteen. Not allowed home drunk and no boyfriends in the house."

"Want me to call you a taxi?"

"Uber." She'd smiled, waving her phone in my face.

"It was really nice meeting you."

"Likewise, but... Go snog Harry. I'll be really annoyed if you don't. Make an honest man of him. Put a ring on his finger and love him forever. Dead romantic."

"Kind of problematic. Harry is straig—" She'd put her finger against my lips.

"Shhh. Don't. Things like that are sometimes fluid. And sometimes not. I mean, I kissed a girl once. Wasn't for me, but hey, she was hot. You never know until you try these things. And follow me on Insta, OK? I need to get an invite to your wedding. Have a new dress in mind. Not a jumpsuit!"

Then she'd gone off in a flutter of pink and high heels and left me standing there like a lump of clay. I could always dream, but I very much doubted her theory would stretch to Harry Thunder.

Not that I didn't want to try.

As we turned down the high street, walking shoulder to shoulder through the deserted buildings, it was way past pub-closing time, and the only nightclub still open was the other end of town. There were a few stray stragglers around, heading home, just like us.

"Would you want to get married one day?" I knew he'd mock me for asking, but at this point, I'd do anything to cheer him up. I loved hearing him laugh.

"Is this what I think it is? Are you proposing?" He was all wide-eyed in mock surprise.

"Harry Thunder, love of my life..." I teased.

"Stop! You need to go down on one knee."

"Not in front of the King's Head pub, babes. It's not classy enough for you." I needed to rein this in.

"There's no class left in me," he said, and he was bloody serious. "And..."

He resumed walking.

"And what?" I asked.

"Not gonna happen, is it? Weddings like this? I have no family. Who would throw me a wedding? My deadbeat dad's bastard kids?"

"Don't speak of them like that, they don't deserve it. It's not their fault your dad was a dick."

"He was, wasn't he?" He looked small, so bloody broken and, in the streetlights, very pale again.

"Harry, stop for a sec."

He did. I put my hands on his shoulders. Reached my thumb up and wiped an imaginary tear from his eye. For a minute, my heart swelled to that horrible state where I was so in love with Harry Thunder that I would have done anything he'd asked. Anything.

Luckily for me, I still had my senses and I got my head together.

"Harry, you're a wonderful, brilliant, cool guy. And very handsome. One day, someone will throw you a wedding, and it doesn't have to be like this. Just you and me and a beach and—"

"You just said you and me. So this is a proposal?"

He had me. And I was an idiot.

"Sorry," I whispered.

"You love me."

"Of course I do, you fool. I'm a gay man with feelings. You're a hot dude with a nice dick. I'm not dead, Harry. You know how I feel about you. But I also know you don't feel that way in return, and that's that. Now let's drop it."

"You haven't even seen my dick."

Thank you, Harry. He was smiling, bringing the mood back to ground zero.

"I have." I picked up the pace. The sooner we got home the better. "Had to clean you up when you pissed yourself at Christmas. Great night."

"Oh."

"Don't worry. I made you wash yourself. Never touched you."

"I know you would never touch me. Consent is a thing. I was brought up on Amelie's school of *How to Be a Rainbow Ally 101*. She was always the woke one at school. Taught me all about consent too."

"Amelie."

"Yeah. And no, she wasn't my girlfriend."

"Did you have one? At school? Anyone I need to look out for and be ragingly jealous of?" *Owen, you dick.* Clearly, I didn't need alcohol to be obnoxious, and Harry knew it.

"Look." He stopped. I stopped. End of the high street. We needed to take a left and not stand here and get run over by Tesco lorries on the roundabout.

"I may be a complete tool and a total twat, and yes I have a definite issue with drink. Do you have any idea how hard this evening was? I was ready to grab other people's drinks and run to the loos and just neck them to make it all go away. I'm not a people person. I have no sense. And no, I fucking didn't have a girlfriend at school. I've snogged people, and yeah, I made out with a few. I think I even snogged Amelie at one point. I definitely snogged someone called Yasmin. I have no clue. But I'm not that kind of person, not wired that way. I don't fancy people. I don't shag around, and I couldn't get a date if my life depended on it. I don't want it! I don't want all that!"

Now he was shouting, and I was completely stunned into silence as he fisted his hair in distress.

"I don't tell people because there's nothing to tell. I don't feel like that about anyone. And the first time I ever got jealous? I'm not going to tell you because you'll make a big deal out of it."

"I'm really sorry," I said, trying to calm my racing heart. "I'm so sorry if I put pressure on you or disrespected you. There's nothing wrong with feeling like you do. People are just people. You don't even have to put labels on what you feel. You're unique, Harry, and you have great friends who adore you."

"Nobody adores me, Owen." He smiled bitterly. "Apart from you."

"I do." I smiled back, though mine was the real deal. "And I will probably adore you forever. Which doesn't mean we can't be friends."

"I..."

There were a lot of words unspoken. A lot of things he needed to say. So I waited. The wind from another lorry gushed past us. We needed to move. Walk home. Get to bed. I needed a shower. I needed a wank. Too much pent-up frustration running through my veins because the way he looked at me—there was something there I couldn't read. Trust. Friendship. Anger. And a pool of darkness that I wasn't sure I wanted to deal with.

"I've never done anything with anyone, and I don't know...I don't know what I want. It's never been..."

"Shh, it's OK," I said gently. "You don't have to explain yourself. I'll back off with the flirting, and you'll tell me if I ever make you uncomfortable. Do we have a deal?"

He nodded. Then he looked away.

"Shall we go home?" I suggested. He didn't answer, but we set off again, slow clumsy steps as we took a left up the road leading home. I followed behind him, my thoughts clouded in a haze of something I couldn't face right now. I was shattered. Bruised. Relieved maybe? I probably had all my answers right there. He didn't want this, and I didn't blame him.

"You know what I really hate?" he said quietly. "I really hate when you kiss Eddie and Joe. On the mouth."

Fuck you, Harry. Fuck you.

chapter nine

Harry

"Harry, just stop it." He was tired of me. I was tired of myself as well and should learn to shut my gob. But at the same time, there were too many feelings brewing in my stomach, and I felt like a ticking time bomb. One that was far too close to going off.

"I know they're your friends, but there's no need to eat your mates' faces every time you see them."

See? Couldn't even control it.

"Enough!" he shouted. "Enough!"

I'd always been good at riling people up, and Owen was no exception. Even when I tried to behave, I still messed with him because it was too easy. I just needed to push those buttons and he would instantly be fuming—on the inside. He'd appear calm on the outside, but I knew him, and he couldn't hide it from me.

This time, though, I couldn't figure out what I'd said to make him thunder up the road like he was now. Long strides with his hands flaying as he tried to speak but was in too much of a state to get the words out. It didn't matter. We were almost home, anyway, and...and...

I didn't know what to do.

Because I did stupid shit when I was drunk, but apparently, I did even *stupider* shit when I was sober.

"Stop!" I said weakly. "Slow down!" He was way ahead of me now, and I had to almost jog to keep up.

"What for? I mean!" His arms were up over his head, and there was frustration written all over his face.

Owen was upset. Or angry? I couldn't tell.

"I don't know how to handle all this. If I said something wrong, I'm sorry."

That was a first, even for sober-me. I was apologising for something, and I didn't know what for, but I had a horrible feeling in my stomach. I shouldn't have...

He was right. I needed to keep my mouth shut and head down and grow the fuck up.

"I think you should think about finding a room to rent somewhere," he said. "Get out and live a little instead of slumming it with me because you obviously don't want to be here."

Oof. OK. He was angry and upset, spitting the words out. He wiped his face with his giant hand, and somehow that made me want to...I didn't know what.

"Owen, just talk to me. I meant what I said. I don't know what I'm doing here, and I—"

"You're full of homophobic shit, and you really need to think what comes out of that mouth of yours."

"And you? You're not? OK, not the homophobic shit, but you're pissed off with me, and you keep telling me to be honest. You said to tell you if something makes me uncomfortable, you said it right back there, and now you're salty because I did? That's a bloody low, even for you."

He stopped. Thank God for that because I was out of breath and running up a goddamn hill trying to keep up with a guy blowing steam out of his ears and glaring at me.

"Why do you always have to do this, Harry? All that crap you come out with all of a sudden. A minute ago, we were having a nice conversation and then all this bullshit?"

"Bullshit?" I shrieked. "That's a bit rich coming from the guy who claims I'm the love of his life and never even attempts to show it. You snog everyone else and ignore me like I stink or something."

There. I'd said it. It was true, but I had no idea what I was doing or why I was saying all this stuff. What the hell was wrong with me?

"You. Are. Not. Gay." He was right up in my face. Staring straight at me, his finger poking me in the chest, and I was leaning back to the point that I almost lost my balance.

And there I was, as always, the idiot in the room, except we weren't even in a room. We were still outside on the road leading up to the house and my brain was trying to come up with another lame joke.

I have to admit, for once, I was impressed with myself because I took a deep breath and waited for him to do the same before I said quietly, "I'm not going to stand here in the middle of the road and spill stuff I've never told anyone else."

He crossed his arms and waited while I rocked on my heels and pulled at my hair. Way to go, Harry. Way to go. Why the hell had I put myself in this situation? I should have just taken off and gone up to London and got a room at a hostel and disappeared. That had been my plan A. I'd never even had a plan B, and how I'd ended up here was beyond me.

Another lie. I'd ended up here because it was exactly where I wanted to be. With Owen Cartwright right up in my face. And now he expected more truths. Truths I couldn't even admit to myself.

Thing was, I said the things that were expected of me. I always had. Said the right things so my dad wouldn't go off on one, so Mum wouldn't have another drink. Put myself to bed so I wouldn't get into trouble. Done as I was told. Behaved like a full-on idiot at school because it was the only way I'd known to behave. It had been expected of me, and I'd played the role to perfection. People expected bullshit. I gave it to them. Time and time again.

"You're so full of shit, Harry. One minute, nice as pie, the next, you're getting on my nerves to the point that I want to chuck you out in the street and let you fend for yourself. I don't know why I put up with you, honestly I don't. I give you everything, I look after you, and what the hell do I get back? All you do is make me feel like the biggest idiot on the planet. And you know what? You're right. I am the biggest idiot on the planet."

"You're not, but please. Can we just go home?"

"Home? What home? You squat in my flat! What do I get out of this...this...cohabitation thing we have going on? You tell me, Harry."

I knew what he was saying. And he was right, as always. I was still behaving like I was fifteen, and...

"You look out for me. You make me feel like I still have a chance...a chance to do something right in this world. I wouldn't be here without you."

Pathetic. Stupid and Pathetic.

"I don't ask for shit, Harry. Not a thing, apart from begging you to play nice. Be nice. Be a nice fucking human being. But you can't even do that."

He was, at least, breathing calmly. He was standing far too close to me, his every breath hitting me in the face. He was taller than me, but we were standing on a slope, so we were level, and I liked that. I liked that I could stand here and he was right there. Eye-to-eye. Face-to-face.

Play nice.

"I'm not good at that," I admitted, and I meant it in every way. I wasn't good at peopling. Playing nice. Being honest. I wasn't good at being a decent human being.

But for once, I wasn't playing at anything. I *was* being honest. I was tired and wrung out, exhausted from trying to hold everything together all day, and Owen wasn't listening to a word I was saying, not really listening. I didn't blame him. Most of the stuff that came out of my mouth was rubbish. But I needed him to listen.

I watched him carefully, watched his face softening by the second. I didn't play nice, but I played all right because he'd always looked at me the way he was looking at me now. There was something in his eyes, his cheeks, the way his mouth curled subtly. He was trying so hard not to smile at me. I made him smile. I always had.

I wasn't cute. I wasn't handsome. I was just me, the pathetic loser in a stained suit with nothing to show for his twenty-three years. And I couldn't give him anything back. Nothing. He was the only thing I had left in this shithole of a life, and I was doing a fine job of fucking that up too.

I didn't know what made me do it. Perhaps it was the surging wave in my stomach. Or the car that passed us by at speed. Perhaps I was just as stupid as I'd always been, and somehow, I'd had enough.

I'd had enough of everything.

The next minute, my hands were around his face and my mouth slammed on to his. He tried to push me off, angling his face away, but I wasn't thinking anymore. I wasn't even considering my inferior kissing experience or how to do this shit right. I just went for it. Kissed him, with all that hair on his face scratching my skin, my lips nipping at his bottom lip, over and over again. His top lip. The curve of his mouth. My nose hard against his. Breaths. Hard, puffing breaths in my chest as I angled my face the other way and let him walk me backward into a garden wall.

Then he was against me, the wall behind us creaking alarmingly as he went full-on feral on me.

I didn't mind.

I didn't mind at all.

I'd always wanted this. Someone to love me the way Owen loved me. His mouth on mine, his hands around my neck, and his tongue.

Fuck. His tongue was in my mouth and mine was in his, and I lost track of which was mine and what was his because this... *This.*

One of my hands was in his hair, the other over his ear. This wasn't the way it looked in movies. There was no finesse and loud sweeping music. No glittery sunset in the background.

This was all raw and breaths and anger and frustration, and he tried to break free, but I pulled him straight back in. My foot was on his and his knee was between my legs, and I latched my mouth to his like some obscene baby octopus because I couldn't do anything else.

Then he pushed off me. Turned me around and shoved me away.

I stumbled backwards, landing on my bum with an undignified yelp.

Not that I didn't deserve it. I did. Because what the fuck was that?

"Don't ever do that again," he said, his voice low but shaking. "Don't ever think I expect that in return. I don't. I look after you because I want to. Because I think you deserve better than the way you treat yourself. But I don't expect that. Don't ever think I expect that in return."

He scared me when he was like this. All low voice and anger. I saw the tears in his eyes as he stormed off, feet thudding hard against the pavement.

It took a few minutes to make my brain compute what had just gone down. I wasn't just stupid. I was a full-blown lunatic. What I'd just done was idiotic on an unprecedented scale. Madness. Insanity.

I stroked my fingers over my stinging lips, my skin still sore from his stubbly beard. The taste of him was right there in my mouth, and I could feel him, everywhere. His hands on my face. His body pressing me into that wall. How it had made me feel still lingered in my blood.

I needed to go after him. Make him stop. Explain everything. I needed to talk so badly that my stomach ached. My lungs felt like they were about to explode. I couldn't breathe, small shallow huffs squeezing out of my stupid lungs.

All I could do was whine, a pathetic sound cutting the heavy silence as my hands clawed at my knees and my thoughts swam in fog.

Breathe, Harry. Breathe, you fucking idiot.

I wanted him back. I wanted him to pick me up and take me home. I wanted to hear his voice—I would even have settled for him shouting at me.

Instead, here came the tears and more wheezing as I curled up on the pavement where I belonged, back in the gutter.

Because Harry Thunder was a despicable excuse for a human being who'd just destroyed the very last good thing he had.

chapter ten

Owen

I didn't get very far, my head spinning in some kind of self-preservation panic before my Harry-radar kicked in and I regained my senses and almost ran back to where he was lying on the ground. There was no doubt in my mind how much of an idiot I was, but I was me and he was my Harry, and here we were again. Me on my knees at his side, him hyperventilating with that terrified look on his face.

I knew he was prone to panic attacks. He'd had one before, after a night out with Joe and Eddie, and tonight was no doubt textbook for what would pull him into one, when he felt so out of control he didn't know where to turn. My nursing skills came in handy, as always. Well, that was what I was telling myself as I dragged him up so he was sitting, held his arm and lifted his chin, demanding that he look at me. Not that I was any kind of level-headed medical professional here, stroking his cheek with my heart racing.

"You've got to breathe slower, sweetheart. Come on. Follow my breathing. Deep breath in."

He barely lasted a second before wheezing out another breath, and the darkness wasn't helping. He needed to slow his breathing. He needed to look at me.

"One more time. Breathe with me. Just like this. In... Out... There we go. Good boy. In... Out... In... Out..."

He was finally back in the game, grasping at my arms, still with all that panic bruising my skin under his fingertips.

"In... Out... Come on, babes. In... Out..."

I didn't know how else to help him. I wanted so badly to lift him up and just carry him home, but despite my size and him being smaller, there was no way I could carry him anywhere. Not like this.

"I'm sorry," he wheezed. "I'm sorry. Please don't leave me. I fucked up."

"Not going anywhere," I reassured him, trying to appear calm, though I didn't feel it. This was exactly what Eddie had warned me about. This thing with Harry. It would always end in disaster.

"I...I need to talk to you," he tried, but his voice wouldn't hold.

"When we get inside." I wasn't doing this. Not here. Not now. Not when I couldn't trust myself to not do something stupid.

"Please...don't kick me out."

My heart bled for him. I didn't want it to—not because he was an idiot. More because I was one too.

It took a while, but I got him to his feet, and we stumbled home, him pressed against my side, my arm around his back. More stupidity. I treasured every step, having him against me, daydreaming like a fool that this was something that meant anything but what it actually did.

Once home, we slipped into step, him going for a shower, me telling him not to lock the door.

"OK," he said, his voice a little stronger. He would usually follow up with calling me names and scolding me for thinking he would fall over and break his neck on the shower floor, and I stood there waiting, but the words never came. All I heard was the shower running and the sound of his clothes hitting the hard tiles.

I made myself a cup of tea and poured a glass of water for him, then I took a shower, leaving him to get into bed. Normal. Everything felt normal when it was anything but, and the unease in my stomach was building by the second.

I expected to find him in the bed, stewing in madness with his back to me. Instead, he was curled up with the duvet under his chin, looking at me like he expected...I had no idea what.

"Look," I said, pulling a T-shirt over my head before turning around, letting my towel drop so I could get into my sleep shorts. I sat on the edge of the bed and tried to appear as if I was calm and in control. "This was not what I expected, but that's no excuse. I got carried away, and I had no right to kiss you like that. And you shouldn't have kissed me either, but two wrongs don't make this any kind of right."

"I understand," he said, being unusually reasonable.

"And I hate that I made you think you needed to give me something in return. Honestly, Harry, you don't. I meant what I said. I look after you because it's who I am. I don't ever expect anything in return."

"Well, apart from rent, which you will get as soon as I get myself sorted. And that I behave like a decent human being."

He'd listened. But I hated the way the words sounded coming out of his mouth. Things weren't right, and I just wanted to scream.

"Anyway," he continued. "I kissed you first, and maybe you're right, and I shouldn't have. But that doesn't mean I regret it. I don't. I wanted to, so I did it."

That stubborn honesty felt even worse. It still made no sense, though.

"I need you to listen to me, and actually proper listen," he went on with determination. "Because I try telling you things, and you don't get it. It just runs off you, like you don't hear what I'm saying."

I got that. I did. But Harry spoke in arsehole-infused sarcasm and weird riddles, and most of the time I had no idea what he was on about. Nothing made sense right now, least of all my stupid head. So, I got under the duvet, sat there cross-legged like a big blob of nerves and then...I waited.

Silence. He turned over and stared at the ceiling. At least his breathing was more normal now, even though he was still on edge. His fingers fisted the sheets, and his lips were clenched against his teeth.

"It's hard to say things. Explain why I'm such a dick. It's nobody's business, you know?"

"Would it be easier if we turned off the lights?" I offered, hoping he would say no, even though I needed the darkness to hide. I felt far too raw, yet I loved being able to see him. Watch him. Share my bed with him.

He shook his head and slowly sat up, arranging himself until he was comfortable. Biting at a fingernail, he shivered a little. He was once again wearing one of my T-shirts, and it made me want to cry.

"Want some tea?" I offered weakly, holding my cup out to him.

He blinked. Shrugged.

I didn't know what to say. What to do. How to make this better. Harry was obviously totally out of his comfort zone, and I honestly didn't know how much more of this I could take.

"You don't have to..." I started awkwardly.

"I do," he said, shuffling until he had the duvet over his shoulders. "I do. I can't do this anymore and...deserve better."

"Better than what?" *Don't argue with him, Owen. Don't bloody make this worse.*

"I'm...I..." He took a deep breath. "I've spent my whole life trying to figure out what's wrong with me. There are a lot of things wrong with me, I know that, but I don't think who I am is wrong in any way. I'm just... Things that normal people live for scare the living daylights out of me."

"Being scared of things is human, Harry. It doesn't mean there's something wrong with you."

"People are scared of spiders. Buttons. Bloody elevators and stuff, but..." He smiled awkwardly and pulled the duvet tighter around his shoulders.

"What scares you?" I asked quietly. And I was scared myself because I wasn't sure I wanted to know all Harry's secrets. I wasn't sure I was ready.

"I've always been like this, and I'm not so daft that I haven't done all the research. I know it's normal, but it doesn't make it any easier to live with. Everyone at school always had all these...crushes and fell in love and had girlfriends and did all the normal things. And I couldn't." He took a deep breath.

"I never understood why, but I didn't want it. I didn't want anything with anyone, and if people wanted to do anything, I would freeze up and run away. I didn't want people touching me like that, and I didn't like when girls flirted and everything like that made me just...terrified. I couldn't cope with it, so I... I'd be me. I would be the arsehole, so people would back off. I never felt comfortable with anyone. And it didn't matter, you know? Because I didn't want it. Didn't need it. I even thought I was asexual for a while, but then you know..."

He smiled and winked. I smiled too. Because yeah. "Wanking is kind of awesome," I said. *Oh, Owen, you absolute bastard.* But it made him laugh, which made me laugh and deflated a little bit of that horrible balloon of anxiety in my stomach.

"Wanking can be nice, sometimes. But it was never about that. I just wanted to not be so bloody alone. I wanted to have someone that was just...with me. On my side. I wanted someone to...be in love with me and then I would be in love with them back, like? Like magic. I know it doesn't work like that. Sex and things like that, though? I've...never done it. With anyone."

"That's perfectly normal too, babes. Being a virgin at our age is actually really common. Not everyone becomes a slut the day they turn sixteen. Just because we legally can doesn't mean everyone does."

"Well, I didn't. Ever. Because I don't feel...attraction to people. At all. Unless..."

I waited, and he looked at me.

And in that moment, I realised I'd always read him that way.

"Unless you feel really safe with them. Unless you have that connection." I sounded like I was reading from some kind of self-help book, but he nodded vigorously.

"There's such a wide spectrum of sexualities, and I don't think I've ever needed to put a label on it like that. All I know is that I'm terrified of other people wanting to do things with me, and I can't stand it when people do things around me. I get really uncomfortable and weird and...I've had panic attacks before when people have come too close and I haven't been able to get away. I've become weirder and weirder and now I'm the...the twat who fucked up everything else too."

"Have you ever, you know, had a connection? Wanted to be close to anyone?"

He laughed. His cheeks were rosy, and it was obviously hard for him to say, but he smiled as he said it.

"Eddie. Bloody Eddie. At school. We were hanging out a lot, and you know what he's like. He talks and listens, and we used to sit in his room and play Uno and listen to music. Just hang out. I lived for those afternoons, and yes, I always wanted to be like him. I wanted to live in his house and have a nice normal mum and sleep in his bed and have him next to me. Nothing more. But it was something that was brewing inside of me for a long time without me doing anything about it. And then..."

"Then he met Joe." I knew the story. I'd heard it a million times.

"I hated him. God, it was awful. Hated the way he was and his nerdy friends, and Joe was everything I wasn't and he was so...like all cute and funny and Eddie was so bloody obsessed and besotted and always wanted him to hang out with us, I ended up hating him too."

"I can imagine. Jealousy is a nasty beast."

"Thing is, Eddie still talked to me. Still let me hang out. I was horrible to him, and horrible to Joe, and we're not going to even mention the shit I did to his mates, but Eddie would just stare me down and tell me he didn't like me very much. I would feel like a right dick, but then we would hang out again. I never got it, but he's always been there for me. Even when he had Joe, he was always there. And I kept fighting him and messing up and being an arsehole and..."

It was horrible to watch him burst into tears. I couldn't bear it, sitting there and not comforting him. But I was listening, hearing the words he was trying to say. He was all prickles and thorns because he was terrified, and I understood that, better than he could know.

"Please don't cry, babes," I whispered. "I know exactly what you're saying, and Eddie is getting married, and you're right here, being his best man. It must be emotionally exhausting."

I was waffling when all I wanted to do was pick him up and shake him.

"I'm not in love with Eddie," he sobbed. Then he looked up at me and grinned through his tears. "I mean, he's this hulk-like bloke with stupid muscles, and Joe is exactly his cup of tea."

I nodded like a muppet, wiping a tear from my face. Fuck. I was so fucked.

Harry shrugged. "Joe is perfect. I'm just the bell end with issues who fucks everything up."

"And I'm a fat slob of a gay nurse with a wedding suit that is still two sizes too small. We're all idiots, babes. Nobody is perfect, not even Joe."

"Is that really how you see yourself?" he asked, and there he was, the Harry I adored. His tear-streaked face opened up with that look of childlike wonder. "Because then I'll agree. You *are* an idiot."

"I'm fat and ugly. That's the truth. Last time someone kissed me was almost two years ago. It doesn't matter how you label yourself, it doesn't mean you get what you want. Some of us are just the ones left on the shelf after all the good ones are taken."

I cringed at my juvenile pitiful comment, but I couldn't help myself. The tears had been brewing since that bloody kiss, and however much I tried, I couldn't hold them in because this was too much. Far too much.

"Owen, I...you have no idea how ridiculously wrong you are. Bullshit wrong. Fuck."
He shuffled closer and reached out, one finger slowly stroking the top of my hand.
"Because it's all your fault. All your bloody fault."

chapter eleven

Harry

"But, Harry..."

He was trying to say something, slobbering like an infant. Not that I was any better. I didn't know how we had ended up like this, crying in bed like the dickheads we both were, but I felt almost high and couldn't stop the words spilling out.

"I know what you're going to say. And—"

"Ba...bes." Oh God. He couldn't even speak.

"If you'd grown up with my dad, you might understand half of the reasons I'm this...emotionally stunted mess. But I'm not confused or having any kind of crisis. I need you to just...understand."

"I don't!" he snapped. "I don't get what you expect me to think of all this. You're the bloke who just bloody kissed me, and... Now what?"

"I don't know!" I yelled back. "I don't have all the answers!"

"Then why the hell did you kiss me?"

"Don't shout at me. I can't stand it when we shout." More tears. Fuck. Fuck everything.

We both stopped and took a breath. If we were good at something, we were good at calming down.

"I'm not that straight," I admitted. It wasn't even hard, and I almost burst out laughing. "I'm not that straight at all. I mean, I've only ever crushed on two people, and neither of them were girls."

"So you..." More slobbering. I grabbed his hand. Because at least that I could do, but I wanted to do more. I really wanted to hug him. And I wanted him to hug me. I think he needed one too, but I wasn't sure if he'd accept it, as he was still trying to speak. "You...you had a crush on Eddie?"

"Yeah, and I think he knows it. We've never talked about it, but you know, sometimes things are better left as they are. It's not like anything would ever have come from it."

"Good," he said. Oh God. The things Owen made me feel. He was so bloody jealous, and I loved that. That he felt that. For me.

"It wasn't like I could go home and tell my dad I might like dudes instead of girls or something because...you know? I would have been out in the street before I'd even finished that sentence. I had no options, apart from to do as I was told. It was always, 'Do this Harry,' 'Do that Harry.' And then all this...this...fucking shitstorm hit, and now, I have nothing. The only thing I have left is..."

I'd never had to tell anyone this. I didn't know what people did in real life. In movies, they made everything look so easy. Calm and romantic. And here we were, two blokes in a state, and I was trying. I was. Honestly.

"I make you smile," I said quietly. "I think me being this...*idiot* who squats in your bed? It makes you happy. I don't have all the answers, and I don't have any plan here, and I don't fucking know shit. But I know I need to work on things and learn to be a better person and get a life and build a future and all that. I'm just trying to figure out how to do it...with you. Because you're right."

Fuck. I was talking far too much and part of my brain wanted to pull the emergency brake, but the other? Fuck. Fuck.

"I want to be here with you because when you are with me, it calms everything. You look after me and you...you..." Another stupid sob. "You love me. And you have no idea how nice it is to have someone love you like you do. I've never had that, you know. I fuck up, and it's horrible, but you still take me home and put me to bed and feed me and look after me because that is what people do when they…"

He grabbed me and hugged me, all awkward and awful, and my arms were squashed against my chest and my face was somewhere in his shoulder, and I cried. I fucking sobbed like the infant I was. Emotionally stunted, my arse. I was wailing into his bones as all the fear and hurt and terror that lived in my chest fought for attention all at once. I couldn't have stopped it if I'd tried.

We calmed down, eventually, and I slumped on the pillow while he tucked the duvet up under my chin. The exhaustion was overwhelming, but somewhere among those stupid spasms in my chest, I fell asleep.

When I awoke, it was morning, the bed was empty, and there was someone banging furiously on the door. I stumbled from the room and down the stairs to find Joe standing there with his fist in the air and a smile on his face.

"Morning!" he said cheerily.

"Did Owen put you up to this?"

Yeah. He had. The guilt was written all over Joe's face. The guy couldn't lie for shit, but somewhere in the back of my mind, I remembered Owen was on the early shift. God only knew how much sleep he'd had, though it was hardly a priority with Joe standing on the doorstep. He was the last person I wanted to see right now.

"Yes," he admitted, "Owen asked me to come check on you, which I'm happy to do because I need your advice. On shoes."

And there he was, pushing past me and making his way up the stairs with a shopping bag dangling from his hand.

"Shoes?" I questioned, following in his footsteps. "What shoes?"

"My latest panic-buy. My mum will go mad," he said, placing the bag on the coffee table and slipping his jacket from his shoulders. Elegantly. I didn't know what it was with Joe. He'd once been the most awkward guy; now he was all sweeping movements and perfectly manicured nails. "You know I was going to wear the black loafers, but I saw these on Etsy and kind of ordered them on a whim. Now I can't stop thinking I should wear them."

"Show me," I said and sat on the sofa. *I should offer him a drink*, I thought, and I would've done, but he'd opened the bag and—

He smirked and held up the gayest pair of shoes ever known to man. "They're very…"

"Gay," I said, stunned into total brain freeze. "They are like…vajazzled Converse."

That made him laugh. And I couldn't help laughing myself.

"Vajazzled. Oh God, please don't tell Eddie. He'll veto them and break my heart. But yes. You're right. They're too much, aren't they?"

"Joe, they're pink Converse high tops. With like...sparkly bits everywhere. I don't think I've ever seen a pair of shoes that scream *Joe Tomlinson* more than these...these...I don't know what to say."

"See? You secretly love them. I love them too, and I want to wear them to get married. With my pink suit."

"You're not wearing those glittery hotpants then? The ones Eddie wanted you to wear?"

"Only in the bedroom, darling. Only in the bedroom."

He smiled and sat next to me, placing the shoes gently on his lap.

"Harry, are you OK?"

There was concern there, and not of the normal you're-such-an-arsehole kind. And that little fact almost made me burst into tears again.

"Fine," I whispered. "Did Owen tell you all that too?"

"Owen's not told me anything. What goes on between the two of you is just that. Between the two of you. He asked me to come check on you this morning, so he didn't have to spend the entire ten-o'clock hip replacement op worrying if you were breathing or not. I'll happily report back that you're alive and well and in the process of making me a nice cup of tea."

"Tea," I said, standing up, slightly bewildered at myself.

"Tea would be lovely, thank you."

Very Joe. He got his phone out of his pocket and nodded towards the kitchen. Yeah. I knew when I was unwanted. I went to make his tea but could still hear him tapping away on his phone.

"I'm not telling him anything about the state of that T-shirt you're wearing," he snarked from the sofa.

"It's Owen's, and I only sleep in it. Just to make sure he never wears it in public."

"Good thinking. You should really take him shopping one day. He has awful taste in T-shirts. Always those oversized things with stupid slogans on them. Hideously ugly. He looks so good in a shirt, and anything really fitted shows off all those nice curves on him."

"He looks good in a suit too," I added, feeling my face flame. I wasn't used to all this, and I wasn't used to being alone with Joe. Also, I was wearing a T-shirt with *Peacemaker* sprayed all over the front. God. Talk about inappropriate.

I could have killed for a coffee. A beer. A couple of shots of vodka. Instead, I put Joe's tea down in front of him and went back and poured myself a glass of water.

"Would you say, in theory, that I'm the gayest man in this room?" Joe asked, casually taking a sip of his tea.

I nodded awkwardly, placing my arse back on the sofa. Yes. Most probably.

"So then, you and I can also agree that even though I was once a bit of an awkward nerd, I'm now quite clued up on things. I'm also not stupid, and neither are you. So if we level the field like that, can I ask you for a favour?"

"Of course," I answered, far too quickly. I didn't quite know where this conversation was headed.

"I would never, ever ask you to tell me something you're not ready to share, so I won't. But as someone who's never ever been in any kind of closet, well, not for long, I can only imagine the horrific loneliness of being in one. So…I'm going to ask two things of you."

This, I had not expected, and I wasn't sure what to say. Small stabs of panic in my chest kept my mouth shut. Fear. I was so bloody tired of being scared.

"First, whatever you're thinking right now, promise me that you know you're not alone. I will always listen, as will Eddie. So if you can't talk to Owen, talk to us. I never ever want you to feel that someone won't understand what you're going through because, God knows, all of us have been there."

There was a massive lump forming in my chest, and I didn't know how to make it go away, so I just nodded. Joe stared at me, angling his head a little while waiting for me to make the next move.

"Why would I…" I started. My mouth still hadn't got the memo to shut the hell up, and I was ready to throw out some knee jerk insult again. Harry Thunder was a dick, and I was so bloody tired of him. "Sorry," I said. "I…I'm not used to…. OK. So, the thing is, I'm not having a crisis. I'm not. I just want to figure out how to do things right. And how not to be an arsehole." I winked. He laughed.

"Good," he said.

"Good," I parroted back.

"Harry, I'm going to sound like an arsehole myself here, but as I said earlier, I've been gay all my life."

"Noted."

"Which means I have a smidge of what they call gaydar. And it's mostly broken, so I wouldn't trust a word coming out of my mouth. I couldn't even figure out my husband-to-be, and even though he's bisexual, he's also the gayest man in any room if you get me. I mean! He finds Pedro Pascal hot. He'd wank over the Mandalorian if I let him. The dude is like a…Lego figure of some kind."

"OK?" I was smiling because I could kind of guess what was coming, and for once, I didn't mind. Bring it on, Joe. Bring it on.

"I know you keep saying that you're not gay, and that's fine. But you're part of our little family, and however that rainbow fits you, you and Owen… It's kind of obvious."

This was where I would usually go all dickhead again, but I kept on smiling, and he smiled back. And sipped his tea. And I drank my water.

"You're really wearing a pink suit?" I hadn't known that. Maybe I just hadn't listened.

"Mum thinks it's grey, same as Eddie's. But hey, I've always blended into the background, and for once, I'm going to be out there, bold and bright and doing whatever I want. It's my wedding."

"It is. You should wear whatever you feel comfortable in."

"Which brings me to favour two."

"Bring it on!" It was strange having this conversation with Joe of all people.

"Can you take Owen down to the suit hire place? Get him something that will fit. I can't bear the thought of him starving himself trying to fit into that ridiculous suit he bought. I want him to feel fabulous, and he won't in that thing."

"I've actually thought about that." I had, it wasn't a lie. "I know a tailor. Made all my dad's suits. I'll ring him tomorrow and see if they can fit him in."

"That would be amazing. But Owen is all self-conscious about it, so… You know."

"Owen is just as handsome as he is stubborn." I couldn't believe I'd said it, just like that. But I had and I didn't stop there. "He's wonderful to me, and I like him. A lot. Whatever that means. OK?"

"Whatever makes you happy, Harry."

"I'm not gay, I know that. But when it comes to Owen, I think I am…maybe. A little…gay."

"It's just a word," Joe said quietly. "It really doesn't matter what you call it, as long as the two of you are happy."

"I know."

I wasn't good with words, and Joe seemed to get that, as he sat there sipping his tea and stroking the vajazzled Converse for a while, calmly somewhere in his own world.

"OK," he said finally, and his face broke into a smile. "Third favour."

"You said two favours. I only agreed to two," I pretend-whined.

"I know, but this is a good one. Mum has changed one layer of the wedding cake to salted caramel. I want to veto it because I want it to be all chocolate. We've come to an interim agreement and negotiated a tasting session down at the bakery. So. Wanna come eat some cake? Please save me from having to agree to my mum's madness?"

"Hmmm," I said, stroking my chin as if I needed to think about it. "Cake, you say?"

"If you say anything positive about the salted caramel cake, I will tell Owen you cheated at Monopoly at our housewarming."

I laughed. "He already knows."

"Rules." He sat up straighter. "You don't scam the bank in Monopoly."

"Joe, I *was* the bank."

"And we want the triple-chocolate layered cake. Don't even nudge anywhere near any other combo or I will buy Trafalgar Square from right under your nose next time."

"You wouldn't dare."

"I would."

I liked Joe when he stood up to me. For a second, I had a flashback to us at school, when he'd been small and frightened and I'd been terrified of my own shadow. What a pair we'd been. Yet here we were.

"Harry, last favour."

I sighed and didn't bother telling him this was number four. "Shoot."

"Don't ever put Owen back into any kind of closet. He fought so hard to get to where he is today. Harder than me. He needs to be happy. Out-and-proud happy because that's who he is. Promise me you'll look after his heart."

"Because if I don't you'll kill me?"

"Shut up, Harry. You know what I mean."

I did. I smiled, and Joe drank his tea and stroked his shoes, and I wondered what on earth had happened in the last twenty-four hours. There was something new in my chest that I didn't quite recognise, and I wondered what it was called.

Hope? Maybe it was hope.

chapter twelve

Owen

Thank fuck for work. That was all I could think as I stumbled out of the hospital staff entrance and squinted into the fading daylight. A Sunday morning early shift was definitely not what I'd needed after the night we'd had, and now my head was a whirling fog of anxious thoughts. If it hadn't been for the constant concentration on the patients, the familiar beeps and alerts, those phrases and commands that triggered my muscle memory and made me react in the right way, I would probably have had to lock myself in the toilet and have a panic attack myself.

The last two days had been intense. Emotional. And I still didn't have a clue where I stood with Harry.

Straight. He'd always said it, and I'd believed it, and then I'd phoned Joe in a panic during my morning break and begged him to go check on Harry. Stupid. I should have rung Harry myself, but I was too fragile. Too scared. Too chicken to hash it all out over the phone.

"Owen," he'd hissed, and I'd heard his frustration over the phone. "You want me to check on Harry? But—"

"I know. You and Eddie keep telling me to stay away from him. He's more trouble than my heartbreak is worth." I'd called him for support but instead was about to get an earful.

"Yeah, I know," he'd mumbled and then stayed quiet for a while. I could hear him getting out of bed, shuffling from the room to avoid disturbing Eddie. "Listen." More whispers, the sound of a closing door and then he continued at normal volume. "Harry has always been Harry. He's a complicated man with an even more complicated past, and it's not my place to tell you what to do or who to be with, but you love him. Even a blind man would be able to see the way you look at him."

"I know, I'm—"

"Owen!" Joe barked, accompanied by the kettle boiling in the background. I wished I'd been there with him, letting him make me a cup of tea instead of cowering in the staff canteen sipping lukewarm NHS budget tea, fighting with a stale cereal bar that was making me want to puke.

"We kissed, and it was bloody awful!" I spat back, immediately regretting my words. "Not like that, but because it wasn't…it wasn't right. And then he says he wanted to and that he's not that straight, and why the hell am I feeling so bloody messed up today?"

"Because you love him," Joe repeated, matter-of-factly.

"We're not even together or anything, and I mean. Love? That's a strong word, Joseph."

"It's not. Not when it comes to you. How long have you known him? A year and a bit since you first met him?"

"Yeah?" My insides were swirling.

"You and Harry have been a thing since the first time you laid eyes on him. That's a fact. And yeah, maybe both Eddie and I thought it was a bad idea, and things haven't exactly been good for Harry. Getting into a relationship was probably the last thing he needed." Slurping sounds. And a deep sigh.

"We're not in any kind of relationship!" No. Or? Joe didn't deserve my madness. My anger. All these feelings I was trying to rein in.

"You're really, really blind sometimes, Owen. Mostly to your own needs and behaviour. You're a nurturer. You're exactly that mother hen we keep teasing you about being, but that's what you need. You need someone to look after because it makes you happy. Do you ever see the way Harry looks at you?"

"He's…needy. And lost." What the hell was I on about?

Joe laughed. "He's never ever behaved like that with anyone else. He's lost, you're right about that, and as soon as you're there, he's glued to your side, happy as anything. I've known Harry since, like, forever, and he's never, ever been happy. See?"

"He's...just...I don't know." I banged my forehead against the stupid tabletop.

"He's everything you've ever wanted. He's that little stray puppy needing someone to love him and feed him and tickle his tummy."

"Joe, he's not a dog."

"I have wondered sometimes."

"It's just...I'm...really scared that this is about to go completely tits up, and I don't know how to handle it."

"I'm going to hang up now, Owen, and go blow my husband-to-be. I highly recommend you go scrub up ready for work, and—"

"Joe, will you *please* go check on Harry? Make sure he's breathing and not doing anything stupid. I hate that he'll wake up and be all alone and stew in everything."

"Like you're doing right now?"

"Something like that." Joe always knew me. Better than I knew myself.

"I'll go see him later. Promise. You will get a full report on the state of him, in his full glory. With pictures. You can thank me later."

"Joe?"

"Yes, Owen?"

"Now I have mental pictures of Eddie in bed that I didn't need."

"See how much I brighten your day? Now, go work. I have things to do."

"I still think you top."

"Bye, babes."

He hung up, leaving me with a smile on my face. He always did—and dutifully brightened my lunch break with photos of himself and Harry eating cake. I had no idea what that was all about, and I was unashamedly zooming in on Harry's face in the pictures. He seemed fine, and Joe looked happy too.

Now it was evening, and I was starving and wrung out from working a full shift on around five hours' sleep, which didn't help my state of mind as I left my bike in the hallway and dragged my sore feet up the stairs. I needed a cup of tea and a shower. And then I needed my head on a pillow and...and...

"Hi!" He stood in the kitchen with a cup in his hand and a nervous smile.

It took a while for me to take in the whole scene, but there was a strange-looking coffee machine on my kitchen counter. The kettle boiled, and he dunked a tea bag into the cup as he filled it to the brim.

"What...is that?"

Words, Owen. Obviously, the words were in short supply. Again.

"Before you shout at me, I didn't nick it. I went out with Joe, and we met his mum for cake, and blimey. Joe's mum? Piece of work. I thought my mum was bad but, well. Joe's mum cares, at least, but she cares about all the wrong stuff, and I was really proud of Joe. He negotiated like we were planning World War Three, not some stupid wedding cake. It was like hardcore, and then Joe was threatening things, and his mum was pulling out the guilt card and...blimey!"

He had to stop and breathe, and the urge to reach out and kiss him hit me so hard, but I didn't because I didn't know what he wanted or if it would frighten him. He'd talked about hating being touched, not wanting anyone to do things with him, and I wondered how much he could take, what I was allowed to do. Could I still hug him? Would he want to even let me?

"So, anyway, I went for a walk afterwards, just to clear my head, and I went up to Thunder and Lightning. You know. My feet just took me there, and it was really strange because they've taken down all the cameras, and the windows were covered in these metal grids, and the bailiffs had obviously been round. I still have the key for the staff entrance, so I went inside. Stupid, I know. But it felt wrong not to. Nothing was there. All the furniture was gone, everything stripped away. Ready for demolition."

"That must have been emotional." *Owen, shut up, you fool.* He was on a roll talking, but he was also wringing his hands and stepping around in a circle.

"There was just the coffee machine in the corner with a box of mugs. And one plant. One bloody plant. The half-dead one."

I hadn't noticed it before, but there was a sad-looking plant in the window.

"Just needs some sunlight and water."

"Plants like when you talk to them, Maggie told me. She always talked to the plants."

"Who's Maggie?"

He smiled but didn't answer. "I bought this coffee machine for the boardroom. I bought it with my money because at one point, I had an income and a life and thought I needed stuff. Good coffee and fancy shit all those things. And today, it was just there, so I took it. I couldn't leave it there, could I? I don't care if they come after me for it, it's mine, and now it's...here. I know you don't drink coffee, but good coffee—it's the best. I even went down to Sainsbury's and got some coffee beans."

"Harry..."

"And I forgot to look for the milk jug. You need one to steam milk for lattes, and there was one, I'm sure. We had one up at the house too, I remember seeing it. I chucked it in the skip, and now I half want to go up there and dumpster-dive and see if I can get it out."

There it was. The guilt. Sadness. A whole range of emotions flashing over his face.

"Harry, why didn't you keep anything? I have a whole storeroom downstairs that just houses my bike. You could have kept stuff. I told you." Me again. Making things worse.

"I didn't want to," he said quietly and came to a standstill, staring at me like...I'd grounded him and whatever he said next, he needed me to hear. I thought about what Joe had said, and I wanted to look away because it was too much.

"I didn't want all that stuff. It felt...almost dirty. Like stuff that had never really been mine in the first place. We owed everyone money, and everything was tainted with the whole shitstorm of last year, and I—"

"Come here," I said. Because enough. Fucking enough.

"I'm not a good person, Owen. Everything is dirty. Stupid. And every time I think about it, I get angrier and feel horrible and disgusting—"

I silenced that mouth of his by shoving it into my shoulder, my hand at the back of his head, my lips against his hair. His arms were tight around my stomach, holding on to me with a strength that brought those stubborn tears back to my eyes.

"You're not disgusting, babes."

"I've done some horrible things."

"Doesn't make you a bad person. I think..." I stopped to figure out the words. "Is this OK? Hugging you like this?"

"Yeah," he whispered, rubbing his face in my chest.

I'd never known how much I needed this. To hold him against me like I was now. To have his arms around me.

"You...and me have a lot to figure out, I know that. But please don't think that about yourself. I know you've made some bad choices in the past, and your communication skills..."

"I need to use *words* instead of vodka, Joe told me. And he's spot on. I used to keep drinking so you'd take me home."

Gut punch. I'd kind of known that but it was still a shock to hear him actually admit it.

"You could have just asked."

"I know. But my head doesn't work well when I'm scared and desperate."

"You don't ever need to be scared and desperate. Not with me."

"There's a lot...you don't know about me."

"And there's also a lot that I *do* know about you. Some good things."

He snorted against my chest, turned his face the other way so he could get closer. Pressed himself against me. Did I love it? Fuck. I never wanted to let go.

"Your tea's getting cold," he said.

Fuck the tea. I had Harry Thunder in my arms. I wanted to tell him that, but I seemed to have lost the ability to speak. However, the growling in my stomach interrupted the moment, and Harry finally let go.

"I...bought pasta. Mushrooms and cheese."

"Sweetheart." I grinned like the idiot I was. "You cooking?"

"I'm not a total imbecile. I know how to whip up a basic pasta. I also brought you home some cake, Joe slipped it in his bag. He's a total cake thief. I've never spent time with Joe like that before, we've never been friends, but it was cool. Really cool, actually. He's...surprisingly fun."

"Joe's brilliant. I mean, we've been mates for years. Never had a falling out."

"Really?" He smiled, handing me the tea. It was already cold, but I didn't care.

"Well, we argue sometimes. Disagree about things. He hates my dress sense and cringes when I ask him about his sex life."

"He says he drives you mad. I called bullshit. Joe is, like, your favourite person ever, and I can kind of see why."

"He's not," I said, then fell silent because once again, I was way ahead of myself.

"Who's your favourite person then?" he asked, grabbing a pan out of the cupboard, filling it with water and putting it on the stove, all while I stood there. *You* was on the tip of my tongue, but I somehow couldn't say it. There was so much to figure out, yet it felt...I could barely stand still, let alone gather my thoughts into something coherent.

"Harry, I don't know what's happening here. You're going to have to help me."

"I'm going to cook some pasta, that's what's happening. Then I'm going to fry some mushrooms and make a cheese sauce because you look like you're going to faint."

"I didn't mean that."

"You're starving. You've been eating those stupid diet bars all day and probably had some tiny salad for lunch—even I would have gone all shaky by now surviving on that crap."

"True," I admitted. Defeat.

"Joe said you're being an idiot with the dieting."

What could I say to that? Not much.

Harry was chopping mushrooms, and I needed to sit down. No. Shower. No. I turned around to leave and then walked straight back into the kitchen. Stood there like the idiot I was, hugging myself with my arms in a shirt that smelled of work and sweat and desperation.

"Harry, you need to help me here because I don't know what I'm allowed to do and what will trigger you into a panic, and I don't ever, *fucking ever* want to scare you or make you feel like you're out of control...but fuck, babes. I really want to kiss you."

He paused from chopping, put the knife down gently on the chopping board and then...he waited. I breathed. And then I didn't because he looked at me and I couldn't do anything.

"Then...maybe you should?" he whispered. "Kiss me."

chapter thirteen

Harry

There was something about the surge in my stomach, an almost pain-like sensation that shot through my toes as Owen launched at me. He'd done it before, just lost his cool and become this...other person who was somehow still him, but his feelings took over and he kind of clawed at me. His hands were around my face and his mouth on mine, and then he slammed me into the fridge door, and yes, there it was again. Warm strikes of lightning going through my stomach and shooting straight down my groin. Which was strange. And embarrassing. Yet...nice. It made me smile under his assault.

I'd spent all my life being terrified of exactly this, the way people behaved in the heat of the moment, because I'd never felt any kind of heat or moments. Every encounter I'd ever had felt awkward, wrong, yet here I was, making some kind of yelping sound as his lips nipped at the corner of my mouth, then my cheek. His nose trailed over my jawline as he licked along my neck all the way to my earlobe. I shivered.

"Is this OK?" he hummed. "Please tell me if it's too much. I've just needed to do this, all day, and I...you're just...irresistible when you're like this."

"Like what?" I was surprised I could still speak and followed up with a gasp as Owen kissed my neck, a soft little touch that made my insides wobble like jelly. What the fuck? I laughed again because...blimey.

"Like this. Happy. Relaxed? Like you have absolutely no idea how incredibly sexy you are."

And there we were. That word. I hated it. *Sexy*. It made me freeze up on the inside, and Owen? He just stopped. Put his nose against mine, and then we breathed.

Fuck.

"That was too much, wasn't it?" he whispered, a fingertip moving down my face.

"No...it's...that word. I..."

"Which word?"

"Sex...y," I hiccupped out. I couldn't even say it. My dad had always used it. Never in a good way. He'd used it as an insult. A put down. He'd used it in anger towards people around him. A joke that had never been funny.

"It's just a word, and I won't use it again. You're just...so pretty. Gorgeous. And..." He laughed, shaking his head like he couldn't quite believe we were here.

We were both treading on eggshells, and I had no idea where we were heading. All I knew was that...strangely and quite surprisingly, I wanted this. Owen was laughing, and now I was smiling, and his lips were on my cheek and things were manageable.

"I like it when you slam me into walls and things," I said so quickly it was a wonder he understood.

More laughter. A kiss on my nose. "I need to eat before I lose my mind completely, then."

"The water's boiling." *Great observation Harry*. Frustration shot through my veins like hot bullets. It was still there, that uncomfortable tightness in my jeans, and his lips were back on my neck and my hands were on his chest, clawing at his stupid shirt.

"Can we? Just...don't stop," I pleaded. I wanted this. I'd always wanted something like this, and his hands were everywhere, on my shoulders and my neck, and I fuck. I wanted way more than this. It was selfish and stupid, and there was absolutely nothing sane about the way I was tugging at his clothes.

"Tell me what you need, sweetheart."

"I don't know!"

"Yes, you do."

How was he so fucking calm? This was when I needed vodka. When I needed anything but the arsehole person in my head banging my fists against his chest.

"I want to do this with you. I'm so bloody tired of being scared and acting out about every little thing. I want to have sex like normal people and want it and like it, and I like this. I liked what we were doing, and then you stopped and I didn't want you to."

Hello, Harry. Aged three? I cringed, but Owen kept kissing me between talking. How was his brain still working?

"We're not going to have sex like normal people...because what the hell is normal anyway?" His voice was so soft and caring, and once again, I wanted to wail like an infant and throw myself into his arms and disappear. I clearly was trying to, with my face burrowed into his chest and him stroking my hair and whispering against my cheek.

"Let's just forget dinner for now, and make out like idiots and see where we go? OK?"

More kisses on my neck, his hands under the hem of my jumper, soft movements against my hip.

"Can I take your top off?" he asked. "Or is that too much?"

I ripped it over my head. Naked. I didn't mind being naked. He'd always been naked in front of me, changing his clothes, walking out of the shower, showing off his body like it was normal. I'd always liked that. I tugged at the annoying shirt on his chest, and he smiled as the buttons came undone.

"If anything is too much, just say so. *Stop* is a good word. Use it," he whispered into my mouth and then flicked his tongue against mine.

That was what I loved about Owen. The way he looked at me. Touched me. Fingertips against my shoulder. Light strokes down my arm. More fingers on my hips.

Love. What a dirty, stupid, silly word. I couldn't even understand it, but he kept saying it, and now I couldn't stop thinking it.

Sounds. I was making them, and I didn't quite know what they meant, but I was hot and cold all over, and his mouth was on mine and his hands back around my face, and then I was pushed hard against the kitchen counter with his groin against mine.

The whine that came out of my mouth wasn't even embarrassing. It was full-on awful. Some kind of humming yelp as my hips moved and my dick tried to jerk against his. He was still fully clothed, and my naked chest was on fire.

"Do that again," he begged, swirling me around until I was back against the fridge door. Grabbing my wrists and pulling them up over my head, he held me prisoner against the cool metal behind my back, my hands tight against his as his hips rolled over mine.

"You have no idea what you do to me," he admitted while I made more of those yelpy, whining sounds and he rolled those hips again, his obvious hard-on jabbing into mine, uncomfortably restrained in my jeans. One of my hands flew down and unzipped. Popped the button. Fuck knew what I was doing, but the relief was immense, and then he ground even harder against me and I truly felt like I was losing my mind.

I got it, I kind of did, tugging at his hair and pulling his shirt over one shoulder. He needed to lose the clothes. There was a hand down the back of my jeans, squeezing my arse. Another yelp and shiver as said hand...fingers...walked their way down under my boxers. Skin. On skin.

"You've got such a cute arse."

"Shut up."

They definitely didn't say those things in movies. In porn perhaps? Not that porn was my thing. It had always made me uncomfortable and weirded me out. Story of my life.

He swung me around again, and now I had my back against his warm chest, his mouth on mine as I stretched my neck so I could reach his lips. Tongue to tongue, warm licking into my mouth competing with the noises I was still somehow making. I was begging. I didn't know what for, but he understood. Of course he did, because he was my Owen. Another whine escaped as his finger jabbed my leg. A hand stroked over my chest, down my stomach. Fingertips along the hem of my boxers. Another hand on my groin.

I grabbed it, held on as his fingers entwined with mine and our hands settled on my chest, holding me in place while his other hand kept exploring.

The finger was still there, slowly stroking between my legs, trailing the inside hem of my jeans. Then he moved his hand, and I held my breath as it travelled towards where I wanted it. On my boxers. Running up my balls. Down inside my jeans, warmth and fabric and heat against the hardness of my erection, then a slow torturous stroke all the way up my length as I trembled and shook and the noise coming out of my mouth was...

I cringed. Panic rose through my veins as wetness hit, slowly soaking through the fabric as his hand pressed against my dick. He could feel it, I knew, and his breathing was all wrong and I pushed away. Turning around, I tried to cover myself up because what the fucking hell was that?

"Harry..." he called, as I stumbled out in the hallway.

"Need a shower," I managed to squeak out.

I didn't lock the door to the bathroom. I couldn't even explain why, just standing there with short, strained breaths puffing out of my mouth. What the hell was wrong with me? Everything, it seemed. I should have stopped him. Run away. The silent screaming I currently had going on was embarrassing enough. Whines like I was hurting when I wasn't and the only thing wrong was the wetness in my pants.

Who the fuck came in their pants like that? All he'd done was touch me, and not even properly. Not even skin on skin. I shivered. Tried to clumsily step out of my jeans, holding on to the sink with shaking hands.

Breathe, dammit.

I did. Barely, but breathing I was. I kicked off my jeans and then dealt with my boxers, ignoring the cold, slimy shit on my stomach, as I stepped out of them in disgust, threw them in the sink and set the tap running. I wanted to throw them away, but I only had two good pairs. I couldn't think. Couldn't concentrate. Turned around and started the shower too. In the state of half panic I was in, I couldn't even finish one task before banging my head against the shower door in frustration.

At least I got in the shower and even managed to pour shampoo on my hair. Breathed. In. Out.

Cleaned my chest. Under my arms. Rinsed. Took the showerhead down and rinsed down my stomach. I couldn't bear to look at myself.

Then there was Owen, walking in and turning the tap off at the sink. He leaned back and stood there while I awkwardly turned off the shower.

"Privacy is a thing," I snarked out. Oh, yes. Harry Thunder was alive and well.

"It is." He smiled. "Save me some hot water, will you?"

This was not normal. This was not how ordinary humans lived their lives.

I waved my hands around in some kind of messy water dance as he handed me a towel. "Are we just going to pretend that this didn't happen?" I half shouted out at him.

He didn't deserve this. I didn't deserve him, standing there with a small, amused smile on his face.

"Babes, what just happened? You want to talk about it? OK. Let's talk about it. What happened was we made out. And it was bloody amazing. Fast, but amazing."

Calm. He was so incredibly calm, and it made me want to cry.

"It was more than I'd actually dreamed of." And now he was staring at me, solid, strong, and I couldn't move. Not an inch. "We kissed. And you're one hell of a kisser, you know that, don't you? That was first-class, full-on stuff-wet-dreams-are-made-of kiss. Then you let me touch you, and that make-out session we were having—it went next-level. Fast. It was the most arousing, brilliantly horny most...I want to say that word you don't like.

That's how bloody brilliant it was. And do you know the best thing of all? Do you, Harry?"

Now he was walking towards me. This huge, hairy man with his shirt still open, hanging off one shoulder. Jeans. Belt. His stomach right there. Strong chest. One brown nipple peeking out.

I had to look away. Smiling. I had no idea why I was smiling because nothing was funny right now. Absolutely nothing.

He took the towel from me, spread it out and draped it around me. Tightened it up under my chin and kissed my nose. Just a small, soft kiss.

I didn't even flinch.

I had no idea why.

"You trusted me enough to let me touch you. And then there was this moment where I looked at you, and I fell even more in love with you than I already am. And that may be a stupid thing to tell you right now, but you are so incredibly loveable. I hope you know that. And I'm the luckiest guy in the world, getting to figure all this out with you. Remember that when you're all anxious in your head."

I wasn't anxious in my head. I was fucked. Completely fucked.

"I...bloody came in my...pants."

Still juvenile. Still me.

"And so what? Do you know how brilliant that made me feel? That I could do that? That you trusted me enough?" He hugged me. His face in my wet hair and his arms holding me together. Me. Little bloody stupid me in this big warm embrace of towel and him and...

"You didn't get to...you know."

"Have an orgasm? It's not against the rules, babes. People have sex all the time, good fulfilling sex, and sometimes people don't come at all. Doesn't make it less good. Other times? Meeeessy."

"Ugh." I grinned. I didn't want to think about...mess. "Rules? What rules? The sex rules?"

He was so bloody stupid. Almost as stupid as me.

"There are no freaking sex rules, babes. What we just did was absolutely perfect. But listen, and listen good. If we ever get to the point where you would let me...you know...touch you...more intimately, I promise you I will mess up and probably come before I even have that condom rolled up my dick."

Another word that freaked me out.

He stroked my cheek. "One thing at a time, but if we never get there, I'll still think you're...beautiful."

I wasn't beautiful. I was wet and shivering and hungry and tired. Exhausted to the point where I needed to sit down.

"We need to eat," I said.

"I stink," he replied, still grinning. "The pasta is in the pot, and the timer will go any minute. I just need to shower, and then we'll sit on the sofa and eat, and everything will be fine. OK?"

Fine? I couldn't even start to figure out what that word was meant to mean. But I nodded and then I reached up and kissed him because he was right there and I could. And because my head was a little foggy and I was still smiling and...

And then he took all his clothes off, and I tied the towel around my waist and went to fry those mushrooms before I did something I perhaps wasn't ready for.

"You're amazing," he called after me.

I wasn't. But I smiled. I wanted to say something back that wasn't stupid, but I couldn't think of anything, so I got on with making the dinner. In a towel with my hair dripping all over my shoulders.

"Babes?" he called from the bathroom. "The thing is once you see my come-face, you may never want to shag me again. Apparently, I look like Shrek when I come, so count yourself lucky."

"Come-face?" I shouted back. "Is that a thing?"

"It is. You should have seen yours."

Thanks, Owen. Now I was cringing into the mushrooms and wanting to die a little. No. A lot.

But maybe there was hope for me. Maybe one day this wouldn't all seem so messy. Or maybe I didn't even know what I meant.

chapter fourteen

Owen

Things were fine. Comfortably so. That initial awkwardness of having been...intimate...gosh, I hated that word, and Harry's honesty was rubbing off on me because there was nothing worse than words that meant nothing when other words meant everything.

"You know you say 'love'?" he said when we got into bed like we always did. I'd put on a sleepshirt even though I secretly hoped he'd let me spoon him *at least* topless. "Do you really mean it?"

"Yes, I do. You know that." I didn't want to scare him with more big words.

"It's a stupid word. People use it all the time. They love clothes and food and TV shows. It doesn't mean anything."

Another reason why I loved him. Because he was a bloody child.

"I don't love you the same way I loved the ham sandwich I had for lunch. Which, by the way, I did eat. The diet is clearly not working."

"You don't need to bloody diet, Owen. You are who you are, and..."

He shuffled closer to me, away from his usual perch at the edge of the bed. Now he was almost close enough for me to pull him in, not that I thought he was ready for that. Today had spooked him, and that, in return, spooked the hell out of me. But I could do this. Because I did love him.

"You're soft, all over. I mean when I do this?"

This was my idea of heaven. Having his head on my shoulder and his arm around my chest and his body pressed against mine was sheer bloody bliss.

"See?" he continued. "You're all soft and warm like a giant, cuddly pillow, and I'm just a bag of bones. That's what my mum used to say. 'You're a bag of bones, Harry, but at least that jacket hangs nicely on you.'"

He fell quiet after that, and I took it as an opportunity to kiss the hell out of him.

"So," he murmured when he came up for air, "you love me more than that ham sandwich?"

And yet another reason. He was bloody adorable sometimes.

"Yeah. Something like that."

"You're so stupid." He'd snuggled into me and promptly fell asleep.

I lay there with a knot in my chest because I did indeed love him more than that ham sandwich. A lot more.

And then, somehow, it was Monday morning, and we got up and Harry made fancy coffee while I made him toast and tried to control myself and not push him against the fridge to see if I could coax another orgasm out of that pretty dick of his. Gosh. The things I wanted to do to him. I wanted to sit him down on the chair in the kitchen and get on my knees and blow him until he screamed.

I wanted to lick those plump little nipples of his. Suck bruises into his neck. I wanted to mark him and suck him dry and lick that pretty arse of his. I'd been rimmed once and almost fainted from the experience. I'd never wanted to do it to anyone else, certainly not to any of my handful of partners, but Harry? I wanted to eat that pretty arse of his and...

Now I had a semi brewing, and Harry was yapping on about having to get there for opening time.

"Where?" I asked, lost in the conversation. Because. Rimming. Yes.

"We're going to go see Brian. And then we'll get your suit fixed."

"It doesn't need fixing. I'll just have to wear what I wore to the rehearsal dinner."

"That's a black office suit. It's a wedding, not a funeral. *Babes.*"

I loved that he teased me.

"It fits. And I feel comfortable in it."

"All good things, but it's not a wedding suit, and this is Joe and Eddie's wedding."

"It's still a suit."

He sighed.

I had no idea what the issue was, but Harry apparently did because an hour later we were standing in a menswear shop off the high street, one I'd never even noticed was there. All dark woods and musty velvet drapes, row after row of fine-looking suits hanging on neat rails and silk ties in glass-fronted drawers. All clearly out of my price range, looking at the lack of prices and labels. I tried to tell Harry so, and he reminded me he was bankrupt, which made no sense.

"Ah. Master Thunder!" said an immaculately dressed older gentleman with a definite flick to his wrist as he eyed me up head to toe and back again.

I knew that look and would've dismissed it, but the gentleman smirked at Harry so clearly had good taste in men—and an even better taste in clothes because that suit was practically spray-painted onto his impressive physique.

"Brian," Harry responded in a voice that sounded weird and not like him at all.

"If I can just start by reminding you that we are still awaiting a response from your solicitors. Your father, rest his soul, left quite the debt in his wake." Another smirk.

"I am fully aware of my father's debts, even though I was unaware he owed money here too. I'm..." He looked like he was about to wobble for a second, but he didn't, and I realised I was holding my breath as he stood up straighter and continued talking. "Unfortunately, all I can do is refer you back to my father's team of lawyers."

Well handled, Harry. Well handled. He was standing firm, digging his heels into the thick shop carpet.

"So what brings you to Hawthe's Menswear, Master Thunder?"

This Brian wasn't being kind. He was cold and pissed off, for which I'm sure he had valid reasons.

"It's Harry, Brian. I'm going to be honest with you, because you're the best in the business and the only tailor I would trust with this rather delicate issue."

So, Harry could speak smarmy. His dad had taught him well.

"Delicate, you say?" Brian was being just as coarse, staring at Harry like he was a piece of dirt.

"This is Owen Cartwright," Harry said, in no way backing down. "Owen is a hard-working nurse for the NHS."

I quietly rolled my eyes.

"He is also my partner, and we're going to a wedding on Saturday, one that is very important to us both."

I didn't roll my eyes now. They were wide open.

"Owen's suit is completely the wrong size. I can't say it any more diplomatically than that, and given my dire financial state, I'm sure you can appreciate that buying a new suit is out of my budget. But I'm hoping you may have time to do a slight alteration, which I will, of course, pay you for. In advance."

Harry, you absolute idiot. He barely had enough to top up his pay-as-you-go phone, and here he was, offering money to fix my suit.

"I will pay for it, *of course*," I butted in, sounding nowhere as posh as Harry.

"No," Harry said sternly.

"And Mr Cartwright has this suit at hand?" Brian asked, looking slightly less hostile.

I held up my suit bag. I'd expected some back-end dry cleaner's when Harry had mentioned alterations, but this?

"Mr Cartwright, if you would be so kind as to step into our changing area to the left and don your suit, I will be with you shortly to see what we're dealing with."

He nodded towards a curtained-off area, and I did as I was told. Brian wasn't a man to mess with. The thick velvet curtain drawn, provided privacy, but I could still hear every word being said on the other side, where Brian was laying into Harry.

"...valued customer to this establishment, but if I'd had the final say, we would have barred your father years ago. Douglas Thunder was a homophobic arsehole and a manipulative bastard. The amounts he scammed us out of are not easily written off, whatever you may think, having the nerve to turn up here asking for service."

I was half expecting silence, but Harry answered calmly and assertively, and I was so bloody impressed I wanted to run out and applaud. There and then. Instead, I stepped into my suit trousers and took a deep breath as I attempted to button them up. *Just.* I would be able to stand and partially breathe, wearing them, as long as I never sat down or ate a single thing.

I unbuttoned in defeat, feeling disheartened. Embarrassed. In what universe had I ever thought I would fit into these?

"You were always telling Dad that he looked a million pounds in the suits you made him. Always a million pounds. It's just an expression, I know, but Owen here is the kindest man I have ever met. If anyone deserves to look a million pounds in a suit, it's him. I know my dad fucked over half this town, and I make no apologies on his behalf. Zero. He deserves all the vitriol he still gets, but at the same time..."

I stepped out, looking like a bloody clown in a suit that had once been two sizes too small. Now it looked more like three.

"Dear God!" Brian uttered.

Harry looked crestfallen. Defeated. Yeah, I didn't blame him. I had no idea what I had been thinking, buying this...monstrosity six months ago.

"It was never going to fit, was it?" Harry said, sounding more concerned than anything. Brian remained silent, while I shuffled uncomfortably.

"I'll go change," I suggested.

"Take the jacket off," Brian suggested, walking up to me. "No, take the trousers off too. Get rid."

He stood there eyeing me up. Circling me like a vulture.

"What I want to apologise for," Harry continued calmly like I wasn't standing half naked in the middle of the shop, "is anything my father said that offended you and your colleagues. I agree with your comments wholeheartedly. My father was not a kind or accepting man. He was full of prejudice and fear, and if I can take anything, anything at all out of this situation, Brian, it's that I have the chance to apologise to you for him putting you through the experience of having to deal with him—and myself, for that matter, because I was no better. Nobody deserves to be treated the way my father treated people."

"Save your words, kid." That didn't sound like Brian at all. "What's this wedding you're going to again?"

"The Tomlinson/Sumner Wedding. Saturday," I filled in.

"I see. Well, then, Mr Cartwright."

"Yes?" I mumbled. I didn't know where to look, standing there being stared at like a mannequin.

"You and Master Thunder?"

"He's an adult. Mr Thunder. And yes. He's my partner." I loved saying that. And Harry looked proud, beaming from ear to ear.

"My apologies. The little shit was always Master Thunder. Company policy."

Brian had a sense of humour. Who would have thought? He disappeared off into a corner, returning with a light-grey jacket.

"You're wearing the slate Hugo Boss three-piece we fitted you for the Hussain wedding, am I right? Last fall's purchase?" he said—to Harry, I assumed.

Harry nodded. I had no idea what either of them were on about and just went along with it as I was manhandled into the jacket and its matching pair of trousers and strangled with a tie that probably cost more than my house.

"It's perfect," Harry breathed as I turned and cautiously took in my reflection in the full-length mirror. "You look gorgeous, Owen. But out of my budget. In a dream world?"

I did. Even I had to admit that. The jacket hugged my chest and buttoned perfectly over my stomach. The trousers left room for me to breathe, and the tie was stunning.

"Mr Thunder, I'm going to offer you a deal. A one-time offer. Only because I know Jane Tomlinson, and we simply cannot have Mr Cartwright wear anything else but this. Also because I will always gladly dress any members of our community. If you see what I mean." Brian offered an awkward smile.

Harry looked a little bemused.

"You have this ensemble, including a shirt and tie, on loan until Sunday lunchtime. I will expect it back in perfect shape, noon sharp. Now, we need to get you fitted for a proper shirt, Mr Cartwright."

"How much?" Harry asked quietly. "That would be," he swallowed nervously, "very kind."

"As I said," Brian said coolly, "it's always an honour to dress the community. All I ask in return is that you let me donate Mr Cartwright's ill-fitting excuse for a suit. Hawthe's Menswear has a longstanding charity partnership who would make good use of it. And remember, apart from selling bespoke suits and high-end fashion, we also run a thriving hire business, and we hope you, Mr Cartwright, will come back and let us ensure you always look..." he laughed, looking at Harry, "a million pounds."

"He does look a million pounds, doesn't he?" Harry smiled. I loved it when he smiled. It suited him and was a world away from the Harry I'd met a year ago, the one who'd been a grey, nervous mess of anger.

I thanked Brian profusely when I left with the rental suit. Standing outside the shop while Harry lingered inside, my reflection in the shop window was anything but flattering. My jacket was old and worn, the shirt underneath way past its best. I was also quite sure I'd gained another stone in the past six months. Who was I kidding? I'd never been a clothes hanger, and never would. I'd always be me, and that ridiculous, too-small suit—I'd only bought it in a moment of madness when I thought I should lose weight to impress Harry.

Joe had been right all along. I'd been stupidly in love with the idea of me and Harry since forever, and what kind of fool was I, trying to be anything else but me? This was me. Messy and slightly unkempt. Big and loud. I was way past trying to impress Harry and make him like me. We were way, *way* past that, and the realisation made me smile. I had a sudden urge to tell Harry that I loved him. Really loved him. Properly. With all the shit we'd gone through, I thought maybe he loved me a little bit back, flab and all, because he hopped down the step from the shop and wrapped his arms around me.

"Everything OK?" I asked.

"Tried to get him to let me pay. He wouldn't. Said I'd paid enough growing up with Douglas Thunder as a dad, and then he said that just this once, he'd be my fairy godfather so you and I could be the belles of the ball. He said that! But just until Sunday. Lunchtime. On the dot."

"OMG, babes!"

"He also said Mrs Tomlinson is a pain, but she does his taxes, so anything to keep Mrs Tomlinson happy, he will always support."

"Small town." I sighed.

"Everyone knows everyone's shit."

"Yup."

"Did I do well?" He looked like an excited child.

"You did better than well. I love the suit. Love it."

"It's the same as my grey one. And I have that tie. So we will look all..."

"Like a couple?"

"Well, we are." He looked so sincere, and I kissed him. Right there in the street. "You told Brian, so..."

"Did you mind? That I told him?"

"No," I said, tracing his jaw with my finger. "Why would I ever mind? I'm so bloody proud of you."

"Good." He grinned. "And anyway, I intend to pay the full rental cost of that suit. Because I never *ever* want to owe anyone in this town anything. Ever again. I didn't know we owed Brian money too. I mean, is there anyone in this town who doesn't hate me? Fuck. I almost had a bit of panic in there. So, I'll pay for it on Sunday. Don't fight me on that. I need to. And you looked so handsome in there. Partner," he said the last word softly, like he was trying it out. A word that meant something. At least to me. I think he liked it.

"I love you," I said. "I bloody do. More than I love the pub lunch I'm about to treat you to."

"Oh," he mocked me. "That's a very couple-like thing to do."

"I'm taking my boyfriend out for lunch. And after that? I might take you home and perhaps treat you to my come-face."

He laughed. Thank God. I did love him. Properly. God help me, I did.

chapter fifteen

Harry

My stomach was full of food and my head was full of anxious gnats again. I couldn't quite put words to what I was feeling, but it was all spinning around in my head. I was obsessed with all the bloody words now, saying far too many of them, and it made me antsy. Especially now, when I was wandering aimlessly around town after Owen ditched me to go to work. Late shift. Wouldn't be home until after midnight, which meant I would have to spend the whole evening on my own.

I didn't like being on my own. Not anymore.

I stayed in town, skulking over to the Job Centre with some half-felt determination to sign up for...I didn't even know what. I needed to get a job. But the girl on the desk was someone I had absolutely, definitely gone to school with, and there was no way I was strong enough to go up and spill truths and needs out to her. Not today.

My feet knew this town, though, and walked on their own, and I found myself outside Eddie's office with a grin on my face. I liked it here, a smart office housed in a scruffy old building, but the receptionist was nice and just waved me through. Today, though, the entrance was empty and deserted, so I went through to where Eddie sat at his desk in his little office with a frown on his face, jabbing his keyboard like it was the enemy.

"Hey," I said casually, throwing myself down in his visitor's chair. His face lit up. Someone could come in and offer Eddie crap on a plate, and he would still stand up and shake their hand. Not that he stood up and shook mine. He just grinned.

"Hey, yourself."

I wanted to say something. Offer to go and find that awful staffroom with the grotty old kettle and instant coffee. I should have bought him a tray of doughnuts. These IT people went nuts over anything coated in sugar.

"You OK?" Words that meant nothing.

"A bit pissed off, to be honest," Eddie grunted. "Just got off the phone with Sarj. Dude, we're days away from the wedding and now he's not coming. Something vague about schedules clashing and shit. I can smell bad excuses a mile off. He's got a new girlfriend, and I'm pissed off."

"What?" It wasn't the first time Sarj had let us down. And yeah, Sarj had a huge family with expectations and traditions and whatever reason he had to cancel. People did shit things and other people over thought things. I knew it well.

"Riled me right up, that." Eddie shook his head.

"More cake for us," I said, and we both tried to smile. I wasn't good at faking anything, though, and neither was he.

He got up, closed the door, and sat himself back down, then leant forward with his hands folded. Stared at me.

"Sorry about Sarj, mate," I said weakly. "I know you wanted him there."

"Doesn't matter now, does it?"

Hurt. I bloody hated it. Hated that people did things that hurt others. I did too, sometimes without even realising.

"What's up with you then, mate? If you're here to tell me you're not coming, I will strangle you. Honestly, Harry." Trust Eddie to read me like an open book.

"Everything," I said. That was the closest thing to the truth I could muster. "Apart from that you will have to put up with me coming to the wedding."

"Good," he said. "The rest? Break it down." Very Eddie.

"Fixed Owen's suit," I said. Calmly.

"Excellent. Good job."

"Still haven't written a speech."

"Don't. You know you don't have to do any kind of speech. Cringe City, those kinds of weddings. Just scrap it. All of it."

"Jane has me down for the first speech after dessert."

"I've vetoed the whole speech idea. Just stand up and say cheers. That's all I want." He grimaced. "Although no alcohol for you. Please. You're doing so well, mate. Joe and I are proud of you. Very, very proud."

"You sound like you're my parents." I grimaced back. "My very young, gay parents."

"We'll adopt you. Joe will be thrilled."

He was stupid. He always had been.

"Imagine that. You go to adopt and get me. Twenty-three and counting with issues and a drink problem."

"I think," his voice was all smooth and quiet. "I think I would have had a heart attack. But we would have loved you. All of you. Even that bullshit attitude of yours."

What did I say to that? I shrugged.

"After the wedding," Eddie waffled on, "we're signing up to adopt a kid. I don't think either of us are really ready for babies, but we need to start somewhere, and it could take years before we get anywhere near having a family. I want to be a dad, however that will look, and Joe will be the best parent ever."

"That sounds...nice." It sounded terrifying.

"I know it's early days, but please think about it because if you ever decide to go down that route, you will make the most brilliant dad. Any kid who's lucky enough to become your child will be the most loved child ever. I won't mention it again, but there it is."

"Kids," I huffed out.

"Exactly. Family. One day." He looked a bit terrified himself.

"Eddie. Can I ask you something?" Honesty was my new vice. But words, bloody words. Tripping me up and causing my head to go all foggy.

"Shoot. But if it's about a job, I still have nothing. They had to let Charlotte go last week. Times are hard. If you want to be our new receptionist for no wage and free bad coffee, the offer still stands."

"Not funny," I muttered.

"I know." He was back to being serious.

"Why did you ask me to be your best man?" Here I went again. Words. Too many of them. "You should have asked Kim."

"Joe asked Kim. Kim absolutely refused. He's obsessed with being our videographer and didn't want any other duties to interfere with that. You know what Kim's like. And to be honest, even Kim said Owen was the man for the job, and he's right. There are no hard feelings there, and Owen is the right guy."

"But why me? You have all these mates, nice blokes. Better people. I don't get it. And what the hell would I say in a speech? Hello, everyone? I'm Harry, the guy who made Eddie and Joe's life hell for a few years?"

"A few years?" He sighed. "OK." Eddie shuffled on his seat and leant back, crossing his arms. "I've said it before and I'll no doubt say it again. There are friends. Mates. Colleagues. People you kind of know. People you follow on Insta. People who follow you back. People you have no idea who they are but who keep popping up on your feed."

"Yeah. I know."

"Then there's family. And then there are people like you and me. We have known each other forever. Harry Thunder and Eddie Sumner. We went to the same playgroup. I shat in your paddling pool. Mum was mortified. You broke my first bike. I fell out of your tree house."

"That tree house was awesome."

"Broke my arm. I still have a phobia of tree houses."

I laughed. It wasn't funny, but it kind of was. I remembered it well.

"You cried so hard."

"It bloody hurt, Harry!"

"I know."

"You came to see me at home the next day. Brought me your comic collection."

"You were always jealous of my comics."

"I still have them. They're in my office at home."

"So you asked me to be your best man because I gave you my comics?"

That made him smile for real. And me too.

"Tell me, honestly. How many of the lads from school do you still talk to? Say, like Sarj. Chris. What was his name? That, dickhead...Archie. Archie Hamilton?"

"None of them."

"There you have it. People who you grow up with, most of them drift away, and it's just the way things are. People grow. Move. Find new people. Forget you exist. Well, maybe not, but apart from the odd message at Christmas, I don't speak to anyone. And Dan—you know? The guy from uni who I shared a dorm with for three years, and we went island hopping in Greece and went to that big rugby final down in London? Really nice guy. Then he got engaged and didn't invite me and Joe to the wedding. And do you know the excuse he gave me? It would upset his grandma to have a same-sex couple there."

"I remember." It had upset me too. "Fuck his grandma. And fuck bloody Dan for not standing up to his family." I felt like a fraud even saying that. "And fuck myself for not standing up to mine."

"You did, though, in the end, Harry. Don't even think you didn't. You're the strongest person I know. Apart from Joe. You always think you're the idiot in the room, and you're not. You're that one person who's always been there for me. Anything I've asked. If I needed company, you'd turn up. If I feel like a games night, you're there knocking on the door before I've even hung up the phone. Straight away. You're the only one who came to visit me when I was at uni. And you still do. I ring and you turn up. Even when I don't ring you, you still turn up. Because you're that guy. And I appreciate that. And that's why you're my best man. Because I don't trust anybody else to actually turn up and do the job. I know you always would. And I appreciate it. I really do."

There was a huge lump in my chest. I wasn't going to sit here and sob. Not in front of Eddie.

"Thanks," I whispered because I didn't trust my voice to hold.

"I know we've had our moments. Stupid fights. Fallouts."

"You beat me up real good that one time. Remember?"

"You gave me a black eye. Twice."

Silence. Maybe for too long, but it was a comfortable one.

"And I know you had a crush on me. I didn't know at the time, but now, looking back—"

"Shut up." I cringed and tried hard to disappear through the back of the chair.

"No." He grinned. "We had a thing. Fact."

"You and I *did not* have a thing."

"We did. And then I met Joe."

"And everything went wrong."

I wasn't wrong. He chuckled.

"I think we should decide not to mention that, ever again."

"Amen," I said in relief. "Shut up, Edward."

"Shut up, yourself." He laughed. "So, this thing with Owen. Good?"

"Yeah." I shuffled in my seat. *Don't go there Eddie. Don't.*

"Harry Thunder. Out and proud?" Damn. He went there.

"Owen and me. We're good. And please don't turn it into anything other than what it is. I'm not ready for that, but yeah. It's good."

"If you need any advice, I mean, sex and things, ask, OK? I wish I'd had someone to ask when Joe and I first started getting intimate..."

"Eddie. Too much information."

"Sorry. I'll just say one thing. Lube is your new best friend."

"Eddie," I warned. "Shut the fuck up."

"Nope. I know you find all this awkward as anything, but trust me on this. Ask questions. And talk to Owen. Because if you don't know what the hell you're doing down there, you can really hurt each other. I speak from experience."

I said nothing. Because. *Shut the fuck up, Eddie!*

"Lube is essential. Order yourself some toys. Plugs and stuff. Owen will know because he and Joe talk far too much. And don't go all stupid when it comes to bottoming because when it's done right... It's not for the fainthearted, but it's damn good. Get yourself some good dick. Life-changing."

I felt ready to faint. Seriously.

"Eddie. Don't ever speak of this again. Ever. Too much." My voice was a low growl.

He just grinned. "Get out, Harry. Go home. Work on that speech. Gotta give people something to remember, eh?"

"Hi, I'm Harry. I once beat up the groom. Cheers?"

"Something like that. Now I have a Teams meeting in five minutes, so get out of my sight. Oh, bring me a cup of tea, will you? Two sugars."

I gave him the middle finger. Got up. Went down the hallway and made him a bloody tea. In that rainbow mug that I took great pleasure in placing next to him on his desk.

"Thank you, Mr Thunder," he said politely, smiling at the screen.

"Anything else, Mr Sumner?" I smarmed out.

He gave me the finger back. Off screen.

I closed the door behind me. Quietly.

Fuck off, Mr Sumner. Fuck right off.

Then I smiled all the way home.

chapter sixteen

Harry

This has been a good day, I thought to myself, and then I chuckled because that was such an unusual feeling. A good day? Hadn't had one of those for...I couldn't remember the last time. Bad days? I remembered all of those. But today?

I felt something, and perhaps happy was pushing it a bit, but there was a calm inside of me that soothed the constant anxiety I had lived with for so long.

Calm. At peace. Again, those words felt too strong. I was ashamed of everything that I still was. Ashamed of who I'd always been. I wasn't out and proud. I was still hiding, trapped inside who I was. At the same time, I was totally hung up on the fact that Joe had said I was obvious. That had hurt more than it should have because I'd always thought I knew how to mask things well. And then I'd remember that nobody else had been surprised at anything I'd done in the past weeks, which was also slightly alarming. I'd expected shocked faces, hurtful words. At least disbelief. I'd never been like Joe—or Eddie for that matter. Owen had rainbow stickers on his bike. The guy had never hidden a thing.

He was obvious. Me? I was the kind of guy who shouted the loudest while trying to blend into the wallpaper.

I chuckled again. Maybe I *was* obvious and just never realised.

The streets were showing their best side in the late evening sun, shoppers milling around and some busker with a violin trying to belt out something that was hurting my ears. I walked on, hands in my pockets, taking long leisurely strides, letting the sun warm my face. I'd only popped out to get some more milk, but walking did me good. Just getting out of the house for a bit. Also, I'd chucked all the sheets in the washer, like the proper adult I pretended to be, and it would be at least another two hours before I could remake the bed and pass out. Another five, at least, before Owen would be back. I couldn't even text him, since he'd be in the operating room working. I was starting to learn his schedule. Memorising his work shifts like a lovesick fool. Once I got myself a job, that would be the first thing I would buy. A spare set of those white sheets so we could change the sheets like proper grown-ups. I loved those sheets. And the bed. And Owen's ridiculously fluffy pillows.

Love. Fucking stupid word.

I'd thought a lot about this. Being happy. I didn't quite get it, and I wasn't at all convinced that this was something that would last because nothing ever did. What I did know was I wanted it, and if I knew one thing, if I'd learnt anything in this shitty life of mine, it was that if you wanted something, you fought for it. Perhaps not in the way I'd always done it because my fists and anger would be no good here. I needed something else, and I honestly had no clue where to start digging for it.

"Harry?"

Oh, hell.

"Harry, darling."

I'd stopped in the middle of the road and almost got flattened by a cyclist, who hurled some well-deserved abuse at me as my mother stood on the pavement, staring at me like I was an annoyance.

"Mum," I said politely, but what the almighty fuck?

"Come here, let me have a look at you. What *are* you wearing?"

I was wearing clothes. Normal clothes. And one of Owen's old hoodies. It was nice. I liked it. And somehow my mother didn't deserve a response to that insult. Not that I knew what to say as she pinched my arm and kissed the air, miles away from my actual face.

"What are you doing here? I left you messages." I couldn't help whining. I'd left so many messages, and here she was while my phone had remained silent.

"Aww, you know, I had to briefly jet back. Slight misunderstanding with the tax man, and Johan thought it would be better if I showed my face before Interpol came knocking on the door. These things can quickly get out of hand, but Johan is nipping it in the bud. Just a minor annoyance. I was going to go up to the house—"

"Who the hell is Johan?" I shrieked. I was losing my cool, my hands shaking at something that felt inevitable, pain shooting through my palms as I clenched my fists.

"Harry! Mind your words. No need to be so uncivilised. Johan has been very good to me.

"And what house, Mum? The house is gone, you know that, right?"

"Keep your voice down. We're staying with one of Johan's daughters while we're in town. She has this beautiful house up Chattenden, and—"

"Mum, *I'm* your son." I wasn't going to cry. Fuck that. What the hell had happened to me? I never cried, and now I was swallowing feelings like it was normal. It was anything but.

"Quiet child, we're in public." Mum looked positively scandalised. And my anger was brewing, flashes of lightning in my vision as I tried to breathe. Breathe. Fuck. I was no good at this. Absolutely useless.

"I can't believe you let the house go," she muttered with more than a hint of annoyance.

"I've left messages, Mum. So many messages. And you just left me with all this...this...fucking disaster to deal with."

"Oh, shush. Douglas was right. He always said you were too weak to handle the company."

I saw red. But what the hell was I supposed to do?

"You took...like all the money, Mum. The art, the bonds, the jewellery," I hissed out. Petty AF, but she had. "And the house in Tenerife."

"Twenty years of marriage to your father, Harry. Don't you dare. I deserved everything I took."

"And what about me? What did I deserve?"

"Well, nothing, dressed like that." She huffed in disgust, backing away from me.

We were now attracting a small audience. Fuck. Fuck that. Fuck it all.

This was when I was supposed to walk away. Stick fingers up in the air and have some pride.

No, this was when I was supposed to stick up for myself. Stand up and be a man. Deal with twenty years' worth of bloody insanity.

"Meredith was asking about the ashes," Mum continued on like this was normal, digging in her handbag for something. "She tried to collect them from the undertaker's, but apparently, you'd already picked them up. Douglas wanted to be scattered on the family estate. If you could get in touch with her and sort it out, it would be much appreciated."

Insanity, it was insanity all right. I wanted to shout. Scream. Throw it all in her face. Push her away from me. I wanted this to be over. The last year, the pain, the hurt, the anger and all the freaking pressure that had been left for me to handle, all of it was steaming out of my ears, my shoulders spasming in pain as I spun around like the idiot I was. She hadn't spoken to me for over a year, and I was right here, right fucking here, and all she wanted was Dad's bloody ashes?

Yet I couldn't stand up for myself, not even in the middle of the street with my mum glaring at me. I just couldn't. I had nothing to say. Nothing to add. I didn't know what I'd expected. That I could just go on living here and pretend I had a new life? That life would just let me get on with it and be happy and have Owen and watch Eddie and Joe get married and then...

Then what?

"I can't do this. I can't. Get out of my life."

"Harry!" Mum gasped, backing away further. "Calm down."

"You can tell Aunt Meredith to go fuck herself."

She seemed to suddenly shrug off any sense of unease, walking up to me and staring me square in the face, pushing an envelope into my chest.

"You will not talk to me like that. You hear me? Johan will call you, and you will take that call. The initial court meeting is next Wednesday, all details are in these documents. There will be rules to be upheld with regards to what you will say, and then you will be summoned to the hearing after that, one which you will attend. Is that clear?"

"Honestly, Mum. Summons for what? I have nothing, *nothing* to do with whatever dodgy dealings you have. Zero. You can't even try. I had an approved notice of disassociation filed on both you and any of your bloody business ventures. It's over. I'm out."

"You are part of this family, whether you like it or not," she hissed. "And you will do the right thing."

"The right thing?" I almost laughed, throwing my hands up in the air. "What fucking family?"

"Well, being spoken to like that makes me wonder." Mum looked disgusted. "If any of Johan's children ever spoke to me like that—"

"Fuck off, Mum." I wasn't even ashamed. "Fuck the hell off."

Then I stormed off, leaving her standing in the road.

I couldn't think. Couldn't breathe. Couldn't do shit, scratching deep lines into my arms. The hoodie was too hot, my cheeks flaming. At the same time there were shivers down my spine making me shudder as I raced down the street. I had no idea where to go or what to do. How to deal with the maelstrom of anger and fear and absolute shit shooting through my veins as I took a sharp right into the shop on the corner. Almost took out a shelf on my way to the counter covered in the usual mess of chocolate bars and lottery tickets and scratch cards. I stared at the shelves behind it like a man possessed. Which I was. I needed all this to end. I wanted all this to end. I just wanted to disappear and forget that I had ever been part of this earth. I didn't have shit. I deserved nothing. And nothing would ever end. This would just keep coming. Around and around, another fist in the face, over and over again.

"What can I get you, mate?"

"Litre of Smirnoff, thanks." I dug in my pocket for the card. I needed to just not exist anymore. Just for long enough to forget everything.

The first gulp burned my throat. I took it as I stood in front of the entrance to the shop and let the familiar feeling of warmth trickle down my insides. And another. I wasn't even ashamed. Then I set off, walking home. My feet carried me like some out-of-control robot. Another gulp, bigger this time.

I just didn't want to feel anything.

The keys in my pocket burnt my fingers as I shook them around looking for the key to the house. Owen's house. He'd given me these keys almost a year ago. Told me to come round anytime I needed a mate.

I'd laughed in his face and almost handed them straight back.

What a fool I'd been. A fucking imbecile.

chapter seventeen

Owen

The lights were on upstairs in the house, giving the street a welcoming glow as I came up the hill. Everything was quiet and deserted, just dark shadows of parked cars, life having almost stopped, being a little after midnight.

It had been one of those days at work, where the operating theatre had been a hive of stress with complications and a near miss where the patient had been stabilised twice before we finally got everything under control. These things made the job worth it, when the adrenaline kicked in, except now I was wide awake when I should have been too tired to think. I still smiled, putting my bike away, and quietly slid the chain on the front door, kicking my shoes off before carefully walking up the stairs.

Just in case he was asleep.

The butterflies in my stomach never ceased to amaze me, the way I spent my entire days wishing he was next to me. How having someone to come home to had changed my entire perception of having a home. With Harry in it, my house had taken on a whole new dimension. Which felt like a massive slap in the face, even thinking that. Because at the top of the stairs stood...

An empty vodka bottle, the cap off. My heart froze in an instant.

"Harreeey!" I called out in sheer panic.

"I'm here," came the quiet reply, and my heart still fluttered, despite him sitting on the sofa, his back straight, looking absolutely terrified.

"I didn't drink it. Not all of it," he said, honesty all over his face.

"Good," I said, trying to figure out what was happening right now. Good was not the right word, and it never would be.

"I...had perhaps a quarter of it before I came to my senses and poured the rest down the sink. Then I didn't want you to find the empty bottle somewhere and worry. I would have told you anyway. It was all...just too much."

"Babes." My heart was still in my throat as I sat next to him but kept my distance. I wasn't sure if I wanted to hug him or shout at him. He just looked at his hands.

"I'm sorry. I know you're disappointed in me."

"I'm bloody glad you're not flat-out drunk. That would have been disappointing."

"I'm not a good person, Owen. I'm really not. I've done some horrible things, and...and—"

"Stop," I huffed out. This whole scenario was hurting my head. This was not what I'd expected to come home to, my rose-tinted fantasies having been crushed and thrown out the window. This was real life. It shouldn't have come as any surprise. This was all too fast. Too much. Too soon, and I got it. I bloody did. It didn't make it any easier to get my mushy brain to compute. I still wanted to kiss him, hug him, breathe into his neck and remember that he was everything I wanted and needed, and even with my exhausted brain in full reverse, I wanted to let him know. I just didn't know how.

"What happened, babes?" I asked quietly, hoping he would at least speak.

"I...ran into my mum." He was still fiddling with his hands. Every single nail was bitten down to the skin, red and sore looking. I hadn't noticed the scratches before, but they were all up his arms.

"What?" I would never become a therapist. I had the human skills of a bloody slug.

"She's supposed to be in Spain, and then she's suddenly on the other side of the road hurling abuse at me, and then she pulled a citation letter out of her hat, and now I have to go to court and give evidence so she'll get out of some charge of tax evasion. Like I would."

"Fuck that." See? I had no skills. None. Whatsoever.

"Owen, I haven't seen my mum for over a year, and all she cared about was herself. She's never actually taken responsibility for anything, ever. It was always my dad's fault, my fault, someone else's problem, never hers. Never ever did she admit to having made any mistakes. She'd throw anyone else under a bus to save her own skin. What the hell am I supposed to do now?"

"You don't have to see her. You're an adult, Harry." I still wasn't helping. I had no idea how to, as his hands were shaking violently with rage? Distress? I couldn't tell what.

"I'm a horrible human being. I always have been, I'm just like her, and nothing will ever be better. I had such a good day today, and then she turned up and reminded me that nothing is actually good. Everything I have will always go sour, and whatever I do, it only makes things worse because instead of dealing with things, I swore at my mum and shoved a load of vodka down my neck."

"That's probably not the full story, and I think you know that. There's nothing you've done that—"

"Do you remember New Year's? When I was here all that time?"

"Yes. Of course. You were having a really hard time, and your relatives were all over that will, trying to overturn the decision to not give them anything from your dad's estate. Do I remember that correctly?"

"There was nothing in the will, and all that nothing went to me. No money left, and the funeral hadn't been paid for, and my aunt was pestering me for Dad's ashes."

"You picked them up. You gave them to her, didn't you?"

He was quiet. Chewing a fingernail.

"Harry. What did you do with the ashes?" I tried to keep my voice calm. I wanted so badly to hold him, make him see that everything was fine. That I was right here. But he was practically vibrating, his voice barely a stuttering whisper. And God knew, things weren't fine. Where we'd been ahead this morning, now I felt like we'd taken a hundred steps back.

"You'll hate me."

"No, I won't. Whatever you did, just tell me."

"I can't," he whispered.

"Yes, you can. It's just a pot of dirt. It won't matter. Not now."

"It will. He was a human being, and he didn't deserve that. Nobody deserves what I did."

"Harry." I reached out and stroked his cheek. He leant into my hand like he was falling over. A small whine escaped his lips.

"Aunt Meredith and Dad hated each other, and I bet you anything she just wanted the ashes so she could flush him down the toilet."

"I hope you didn't..." I started. What the fuck had he done?

"I was drunk and bloody exhausted, and I was at that New Year's party and then I left. Because it was New Year's, and the whole shitstorm of what was going on was driving me mad, and I felt like everyone was against me. I was trying to swerve the next disaster, and instead, I just kept sinking, and then, whenever I tried to get anywhere, there was just never-ending quicksand of shite being thrown at me. I couldn't take it anymore. I did pick up the ashes, and I didn't know what to do with them, so I'd put them in the garage because I didn't want them in the house. I didn't want him in the house."

"Understandable," I said, letting my hand travel downwards until my palm on his neck, his skin warm against my fingertips.

"I was drunk." He looked at me, and there was so much pain there, his once pale-blue eyes now almost black.

"You were. I remember."

"I went home and picked them up. And then I went down to Thunder and Lightning and threw him all over the car park. Because he deserved to be there, in the dirt. The building was going down, and I somehow thought he should go down with it."

He stopped. Breathed. I breathed with him. We did this thing, I realised. Where we calmed each other down. Deep breaths. In and out. Together.

"Just breathe," I said.

"OK," he replied. At least he wasn't hyperventilating. Just shallow, small huffs of air.

"So now...your dad will...forever be part of the history of that place." I was trying. Trying to make sense of something that made no sense at all.

"It's not funny, Owen."

I hadn't realised that I was smiling. But I was. And no, it wasn't funny. Not really.

"He loved that company. It was like his, his favourite child. It was always T&L this and T&L that and how well the stocks and shares had performed." Harry sounded bitter. Bitter was better than angry. Anything was better than the state of mind he'd gotten himself in.

"And now they get to be together forever." His small spurt of laughter was disrespectful to the max. "And he'll have a giant headstone in bright lights. And people will worship him, visiting his final resting place." Harry was funny when he wanted to be.

"Babes, you fucked up. And I don't really know how to say this, but that was...kind of stupid."

"Yeah."

"But there's nothing we can do to fix it."

"Nope." He took another breath, watching me as I did the same. Calm. We both needed to be calm.

"I don't regret it. That's the worst part. He was a vile person. A really, *really* bad parent, and my mum was no better, I know that now. I spent all my teenage years trying to be exactly what they wanted me to be, and they still couldn't give me a break. Dad wanted me to go to this private school, and I had to sit an entrance exam. I failed it on purpose because I wanted to stay at school with Eddie. I've never seen him so angry. I honestly thought he would kill me. I think Mum sent me away to stay with Aunt Meredith for the half term so he wouldn't." He grimaced, and then he gave me the saddest smile. "You don't want to hear my sob stories. But I do this all the time. I fuck things up and do things that no decent human would do. I can't seem to stop it, and I will do stupid things again. I will get upset and drink and mess up and run my mouth, and I'm so bloody terrified of the fact that I need to go and get a job. I've never had a job. Ever. Working for Dad wasn't a job, it was an absolute shitshow. What am I supposed to do now? Live the rest of my life here, washing your sheets?"

"You washed the sheets?" I tried to look over my shoulder into the bedroom. Yes. Bed made.

"I even ironed them. Kept me busy."

"You're brilliant. You didn't have to."

"I live here, don't I?"

He did. I kissed him, hands around his face and everything, because there was only so much resistance I could manage with him in front of me, wearing my hoodie. It had a stain down the front and was far too big for him, but I loved that he wore my clothes. Loved that he'd been honest with me. I fucking loved him. And I told him so between trying to maul his mouth and kiss his eyelids and getting my fingers all twisted up in his hair.

I only stopped because he was crying, and that broke my heart. All over again.

"Babes," I said quietly.

He sobbed into my shoulder. I pushed him away.

"OK. This is what we're going to do." I had to take another deep breath. Because this was no good. "I'm going to go get rid of that bottle, so when we wake up tomorrow, it won't be sat there reminding us of stuff that no longer matters. Clean slate. OK?"

He needed to blow his nose. Did I have a tissue? No. I took the hem of my shirt and lifted it up and wiped his bloody face.

"Go brush your teeth and get into bed," I said like he was a kid. Which he was. Harry Thunder was a bloody child.

I couldn't cope. Not right now, and it was a relief to escape down the stairs and throw the bottle in the bin. I even found the cap in the sink and chucked it in the recycling. Then I washed my hands. Brushed my teeth. Got rid of my clothes and had a shower. After the day I'd had, it felt like some kind of messed-up rebirth. It also gave me a few minutes to process.

One step forward. A hundred steps back. I was pushing this. Hard. And he was nowhere near ready. Which made even less sense when I walked into the bedroom to find Harry curled up on the bed. Naked.

"Grumphhgih," I said, or something like that, as I dropped my towel in sheer shock.

I'd seen him naked, of course, but not with him splayed out on my bed, looking like he wanted to die. He tried to crawl under the covers.

"Don't you dare!" I ripped the duvet off him. See? If he thought he was stupid, I was no better. Fuck you, Owen. Fuck you sideways.

"Sorry," he whispered, grappling with the sheets as I climbed on top of him because at the end of the day, I was a dude, and he was irresistible. And this, in any context...

"I just...can you?"

"You need to use words." I groaned. "I can't mind read."

"Do what you did the other day," he growled, trying to get his lips on mine and his arms around my back and then he lifted his hips up and his dick was right there, and mine was filling out faster than I really wanted it to.

I'd thought about this. The next step. Seducing him slowly and carefully and getting him used to the things I wanted to do to him. I'd had a stern talk with myself in the shower. Promised to let him rest. Recoup.

Yet here I was on top of him, pushing his wrists down into the mattress and humping the shit out of his worn-out body as my mouth travelled down his neck.

"More," he said, coming up for air.

I squeezed his arse. I wanted to bite those butt cheeks because they were pure perfection. Smooth, round perfection. His shoulders shivered as I licked down his chest. Then I stopped. Because this was madness.

"Don't," he said. "I just want to forget today. Can we just make this day a good one?"

"Finish off on a good note?" I could barely speak, wanting to scream at my dick that was still humping his leg.

"I want to...I need to feel. I want to feel something good, like the other day. You don't have to be careful with me because I need to do this. I want you to...do things to me."

"What things, Harry? Tell me."

He had no idea what he was doing to me. Making me say those words. And how much making him beg me for...for anything...was making my chest flame. My dick hurt. Gosh. I wanted. I wanted everything, and all my sensibilities were flying straight out the window.

"I want...you know. Do it. Properly."

"Those are not the right words." Fuck.

"Don't make me beg," he growled, trying to hide his face in my neck. "I know you're supposed to wait and take things slow and all that, but I know you wouldn't hurt me, and I've waited twenty-three bloody years to find out if I actually like dick as much as I think I do, and you've got that...big thing of yours stabbing me in the guts anyway, so can you just bloody...please?"

"Harry, anal sex is something incredibly intimate, and I don't know—"

"Don't," he said, and there was this sudden determination in his voice that was new. The way his hands were around my face. The way he looked at me. How my traitorous hips just wouldn't stop jerking. He turned me on something stupid.

"I know you know what you're doing. So bloody do it. For me."

"Why?" My newfound stupidity had no limits. Clearly, living with Harry Thunder was affecting my brain.

"Because I need it. Because you do too. Because I think if we just stop overthinking this and...if you let me try...I think...fuck..."

"I love you," I said. I had to. Because I did. And when I looked at him, I couldn't control a single thing.

"I need to feel all of this. I want you on top of me and inside of me, and I want you to do this and you need to come. I need you to come. That's all I want."

This was when I set boundaries. This was when I was the bloody grown-up in this—even the word made me smile—*relationship*. We were two kids trying to navigate real life, one that neither of us had a clue how to live. I didn't know what I was doing. The guy underneath me had never done this before, and I was no doubt about to scar him for life. On top of that, he had a definite problem with vodka that I had no idea how to even start untangling. And the mother-issue was making me wonder if we would be eliminated in our sleep by some underground mafiosos from Tenerife. Yet his mouth was back on mine, and his legs were around my waist and my dick was definitely nudging around in places it shouldn't be going, and could I stop myself?

There was another growl from beneath me as I lost control. Because that was apparently what I did. I nipped at his skin, licking over his nipples as his head stretched back and his fingers tugged at my hair.

"Yes," he moaned. "Just bloody do it."

I wasn't about to do anything. But if he wanted to feel...

There went my mouth, over his stomach, my nose burrowing into his groin, taking long, deep breaths so I could smell him, get every little molecule of musky scent, and the breathing was honestly making me lightheaded. Tastes. His dick slipped into my mouth as he roared. *Yes, Harry. I know. It's good, isn't it?* Deep, long thrusts into my willing mouth as I tried to take him all in. It was too fast, I knew that, and he would probably spill before I got anywhere near an orgasm myself. Not that I wouldn't have one, but he needed one and God help me, I would give him one. Such hardship.

I kissed his dick. Licked it. Sucked it. Moved down over his balls as he squirmed a little, kicking his legs around.

"Harry," I muttered. "Stop. Word. Use it."

"Don't bloody stop," he growled back. "Lick me. Down there."

I had lied when I said I wasn't anywhere near an orgasm. Because hearing him talk like that?

"Say it again," I breathed out as my body throbbed.

"Lick...ahuoooo." *Good boy, Harry.* Fuck. I was going to come. I was, and now I had to lift myself off him and squeeze my dick just to calm myself down.

"You're...amazing." I could barely speak, my head hanging between my shoulders with his hands in my hair.

"Do it. Do all of it. Please."

I wanted to say no. I wanted to do the right thing and stop this madness right there, but who was I to make any kind of decisions here? And then my tongue was back where it belonged as I threw his leg over my shoulder and held him down with his hips skewed to the sides while his knees had me in a vice.

Yeah, Harry. I know the feeling. Nice, eh?

There it was. That soft hairiness between his legs. I loved that there was no stupid manscaping here, and I doubted Harry had ever let a razor anywhere near his lower regions, which was such a turn-on that I didn't know what to do with myself.

I licked, kissed, my fingers holding him open as I got that first long stroke over his taint, that small, puckered opening tensing under my assault.

The sounds coming out of his mouth weren't helping, they just egged me on. He slowly relaxed, letting me kiss the insides of his legs before I headed back, jabbing my tongue against the opening, then pulling back as he panted.

"Fuck you," he was saying up there. "More."

"Gotta give you time to relax. We want you all chill and open down here."

"Oohmpf." That's all he could apparently say when I pushed the tip of my tongue into him. Out. Then in again. Small pushes as he panted and breathed and kicked his leg.

"Gonna use my fingers now too."

"Lu...ube?"

Good thinking. I smiled and he repositioned himself, one leg up against his chest, the other back over my shoulder, like he knew what he was doing when none of us did.

I was prepared, of course I was, rumbling around behind the headboard. I'd stashed up. Just in case.

I gave his arse a kiss, a last lick before coating my finger in lube and smearing it everywhere. I hated the taste of lube, so it would have to be a hand job now, even though my mouth was back on his leg. Small kisses up his balls. A slight shift as I leant over on my elbow and swallowed his dick back down my throat. Well. Almost. I wasn't that good. But his dick in my mouth was heaven, and my finger pushed against his opening as his mouth spilled out a load of words that made me want to laugh. *Oh yes, Harry. I remember it well. The first time someone fingered me open... Yes. Mind blown.* And there was his little prostate, and I slowly stroked over the little bump, making him almost knee me in the face.

"Fuuu..."

"You OK?"

"Yeah."

So he could still speak. Good to know.

I was no expert on this, but he...he was doing good, his arse clenching and relaxing as I carefully moved my finger inside of him, then added another. More sounds. More humping the sheets from me. I wasn't going to make it. God knew I wanted too, but I had to get up on my knees because—

Down, dick. Down!

"I...want to feel it," he said. "I want to feel you."

I needed more time. But then I didn't, and I wanted this more than I could actually put words on.

He wasn't ready. I wasn't ready, but he shifted his legs, and I was suddenly right there, lifting his hips up and bending his body like a doll, pushing his legs against his chest and lining up my dick against his hole.

I had to stop. Breathe. Look at him. Because this was insane.

"I want this," he said quietly, staring at me with that look that once again threw my head for loop.

"I want this," he repeated. "Because...you're mine and I'm yours, and I think..."

"I love you."

"I know. Your crush on me is getting super embarrassing. So stop overthinking and do this."

How could he joke about that right now? But the laughter spilled out of me in relief.

"So, we're doing this?"

"Yup. Eddie said I needed dick. You've got it. Do it."

"Don't mention Eddie. Not now."

"He's hot. But not as hot as you."

"Harry, it's like the ultimate insult to mention other people in the throes of passionate love-making."

"Then stop messing around!" He grinned. "Dick in hole. You have one job."

It was his fault. He made me. But I had my rock-hard dick in my hand, and I put it against the opening, and I didn't even think about bloody condoms as I drizzled lube over myself like mustard on a freaking hotdog, smeared it around and then...

His face scrunched up.

"Do it."

"Not gonna hurt you." I tried to pull back, but he had my wrist in a vice-like grip and just stared at me.

"Do it."

I pushed. Again. And a little more. And he wriggled his hips, and I pushed and...I slowly started sliding in.

This was insane.

The way I held his legs down, my dick moving further inside of him, the sounds coming out of his mouth...were intoxicating. My head was swimming in static.

"More," he said. With determination. There were little pearls of sweat all over his forehead.

I pulled out, added more lube as he whined and cursed me and shouted demands.

Back in. Sliding. Pushing. A little harder.

I lost my mind after that because it was just the way things went when my body took over and I just did what I did. Because he was there. Because I was here.

"I want to feel you. Every bit of you," he whispered. I couldn't understand how he could still speak. I couldn't.

I pulled out. Slammed back in. Out again. A roar escaped my mouth as I pushed all the way inside of him, my skin against his, his dick standing straight up. I wanted to suck it. I wasn't built that way, but I grabbed his hand and made him touch himself while my body moved in some kind of messed-up dance routine, grinding my dick against his insides as my head was thrown back and I couldn't breathe. It was just...black. Darkness everywhere as the blinding surge shot through me, sprinkling the insides of my eyelids with small, twinkling stars. And again. Another surge as my body stilled, all the way inside of him.

I couldn't think. Couldn't speak. My arms lost control as I slumped over him, my face in his neck, his breaths small hiccups, his legs moving to clamp around my waist, trying to hold me inside when my softening dick was sliding out of him.

"You OK?" he whispered softly.

"I think so." *Lame, Owen. Lame. Where are those sweeping declarations of love?* "I need to go wash my face before I kiss you."

"Yeah." He was smiling. I could hear it.

It took a while for our limbs to relax, for me to slide out of him, leaving a trail of sticky mess behind. He spread his arms over his head, stretching that thin body of his.

He still had a hard-on, and I went for it, slower this time, leisurely licks as he went back to jerking around, trying to rip my hair out.

"Gonna make you come," I promised, and he replied with a string of syllables I couldn't make out. But I did make him come, with his dick in my mouth and my hands on his arse and his hips arching off the bed as my mouth filled with warmth.

I swallowed it down, savouring the taste as another spurt hit the back of my throat.

He was absolutely quiet. His chest falling and rising as I lay there with his softening dick in my mouth, slowly coming back to my senses, a trickle of fear creeping in as his fingers slowly played with my hair.

"Thank you," he whispered. "Thank you for...doing that. I needed it."

"I needed it too. We're...we're just who we are. And you're beautiful."

Words. I needed to find all of them. But none of them were coming out right.

"You're mine. You're my Owen," he said quietly.

Those words seemed to fit.

I was his, as he was mine. And perhaps right there and then, that was all we needed to know.

chapter eighteen

Harry

I woke up far too early, feeling like I'd been run over by a bus, which gave me some uncomfortable flashbacks because I'd been there before, far too many times. The only difference was that this time, I hadn't been beaten to a pulp by some arsehole while nursing a hangover. This time...

I had to swallow an embarrassed giggle because I still didn't quite believe in this new me. The one who was desperately trying not to be a dick. I'd been one, I knew that, and my head hurt. I thought I'd figured out the universe in the past two weeks, but I knew shit.

Apart from that I needed a poop and my arsehole stung, which was not quite the morning after vibe I'd imagined.

"I can feel you staring at me," I said, still not opening my eyes. I knew he was awake. And I could feel him staring. It was like...super obvious. The way he was trying to breathe quietly and not move. His legs were twitching, and he was smiling...and definitely *not* peeking at him from behind the pillow.

"Morning, sweetheart."

Caught in the act. But yeah. He was smiling, and the sun was shining, casting a flickering light show across the sheets.

"It's not quite morning. I think it may be lunchtime." I needed to get up. I needed coffee. I needed that toilet. But it was hard to move away from Owen smiling at me, all sleepy and cute.

He was a bloody giant compared to me, but he had become my favourite thing in the morning, hair all over the place and pillow marks on his cheek as he rolled over and stretched.

He had hair *everywhere*. Bushy armpits and a thickly covered chest. Fuzzy arms and legs. I loved the way his hairy skin stretched over his muscles. He had them, maybe not like some gym bunny superhero, but there were shapes and bones and muscle and endless miles of furry skin...and he always smelled good. It was funny how I looked at him and then breathed him in. I'd always looked at people, but never like this. Not the way I went all warm on the inside, simply because he smiled.

It was official. I was a total sap.

I reached out and touched him, stroked my fingertips over his rounded belly, up his chest. Down his arms. He kept looking at me, and I was kind of half embarrassed and half aroused.

I was fucked, and that wasn't just the sting between my cheeks.

"I really need the loo," I stuttered out.

"Well, why are you still here then? Go!"

See? We were totally romantic.

It made me laugh as I sat on the toilet. I'd never imagined life could be like this. Relaxed. Devoid of tension. Just easy where the expectations were featherweight and the feelings were...heavier, but still. I liked this. I liked owning nothing. Having nothing. Just existing and, for the first time in my life, letting myself just feel.

There was nobody telling me what to do or how to behave or which words to use. As long as I kept breathing and using my head and my own words... The thought of that bottle of vodka yesterday still made me cringe. I'd stumbled inside the house and thrown myself up the stairs, and then I'd stopped. Because this house was not an unhappy place, and I'd been right there making it one. I couldn't be unhappy when I was here, in this place, where Owen loved me and everything was just a little bit better. Every day, things became lighter, and I'd almost fucked it up. Hence I'd tipped the drink down that sink and had a childish mini meltdown.

Even the thought of Mum couldn't hamper my good mood. I'd been a total grown-up and called our former law firm and got straight through to the right person to whom I'd spilled some angry facts while they laughed and told me not to worry about it because that meeting would never happen. They were on it and would ring me back next week.

I couldn't pay them and had no idea why they still accepted my calls. But I suppose my life had been their life for the past years, and once you got involved with a case, it was hard not to follow through.

This morning, I felt like following through was, perhaps, the way to go. Go sit in that courtroom with my head held high and be all mature and adult and tell the truth like it was.

"Do you want toast?" Owen called from the kitchen. Yeah. I did.

I smiled and washed my hands, taking a moment to study myself in the mirror. I could feel him everywhere. His handprints on my skin. Ghosts of his kisses lingering on my neck. The funniest thing was that I loved it. I'd never thought I would. It was crazy how things were slowly piecing themselves together in my head. How this me—this strange new me—was calm.

"Babe?"

"Yes please!" I called back. "And coffee!"

"You can make your own coffee. I still can't figure out how this machine works. It says steam on the display, and it keeps hissing at me like it hates me."

"It doesn't hate you, it's just...wait." I marched into the kitchen, and it only occurred to me that I was stark naked when Owen smiled. Like the happiest smile ever. Well, he was stark naked himself, so whatever.

"I love it when you're naked," he said. "I love that you feel comfortable enough to just be yourself around me."

Cringe. Yet, I was grinning back at him, my cheeks flaming. And now there was steam shooting out of the coffee maker. I jumped back, and Owen laughed.

"Naked coffee making is perhaps not my new favourite thing," I huffed, pressing the buttons and trying to shield myself with the tea towel. "You need it on brew. Not steam. Then you set your strength and then espresso or long. See?"

"I still think naked coffee making is *my* new favourite thing." He clearly wasn't listening to a word I was saying, standing there fiddling with the butter packet and burning the toast.

"Toast?" I said.

"Yup," he replied with a dreamy look on his face. "Shit!"

Yeah. He'd burnt the toast. Not that it mattered. Who needed toast when I could just snuggle up to him and he would wrap his arms around me and smother me in the best hug known to man? Owen smelled nice, even with morning breath and sweaty skin. Soft, clean, hairy and—I burrowed my face into his chest—comforting.

Home. I'd had one all my life, but never like this.

"I love living with you," I blurted. I never wanted to leave. This was safe. A proper home. Well, I needed to start paying the bills, but those thoughts were swiftly tucked to the back of my head. Tomorrow. Another day.

"Even when I burn your toast?"

"Yeah. I know it's only been a few weeks but..."

"Babes, you've been living here, on and off, for the past year. It's not like this is new. We fit, you and me. And you know the best bit? The very best bit?"

"What?" I was smiling so hard my cheeks hurt. And the smell of coffee was as intoxicating as the kiss he placed on the top of my head.

"I get to come home to you. Do you know how brilliant that is? Knowing that I will be walking through that door, and you're here and I get to touch you and kiss you? And...more."

"Sex." I giggled. Cringe. I needed to get over myself.

"Yup," he replied, letting me go so he could rescue the new slice of toast that had cheerily popped out of the toaster.

I grabbed the coffee and flicked the kettle on. *Sex.* The word still made me nauseous, but I was getting there. I just needed to get used to the fact that this was now my life. With sex in it.

"I'm going to go get a milk jug today so I can make you a proper latte. Even though it's a terrible invention. Like coffee for babies. All milk and hardly any of the good stuff."

"Don't diss the latte. I love a good latte."

"Joe told me. You only ever drink tea with me, and it turns out you cheat-drink lattes with Joe? Unacceptable. We will change that. But seriously. Half a shot of espresso? That's coffee for toddlers."

"Don't mock my special order. The barista at the hospital even remembers! At least I've scrapped the double shot of hazelnut syrup."

"OMG." I had to laugh. "No. No, no, no."

"Careful, or I'll eat your toast."

"You wouldn't dare."

He did. Taking a big, showy bite out of the slice as I grabbed it and shoved the remains in my mouth like a child.

Stupid. I know. But it made him laugh, and we stood there, him dunking his teabag, me sipping my coffee.

"How did you get...you know. How did you learn to be good at sex?" I wasn't even embarrassed asking. I needed to know.

"I'm not good at sex. I just...do what turns me on." I may not have been embarrassed, but he was. Just a little. "And there's no better turn-on than making someone else feel good too."

"You *are* good at sex."

"Well, so are you. Nothing we've done has lasted more than a few minutes. That's total proof that you're good at it too. And last time, we both came. That's kind of...expert sex."

"We are not having expert sex," I said, but perhaps we were. Whatever, I wasn't complaining.

"I had some...not so satisfying dates when I was really young," he said. "Not bad, just weird. Because when you don't know what you're doing, things can get awkward."

"I can imagine." I grimaced. The thought of doing anything with anyone had always repulsed me. And yet...here I was.

"I met this guy called Colin a few years back. Had a hook-up. He was a little older, a big, burly guy with a massive beard. Super nice. Anyway, he kind of taught me how...you know. Listen to your body, and just follow your instincts. If something feels good? Go with it. And he was majorly into rimming and...yeah. His collection of toys was terrifying. I hooked up with him twice, that's how good it was. Then he met someone and disappeared off Grindr, and that was it."

"Eddie said we needed toys." Now I was embarrassed. And whoever Colin was, I didn't know if I should rage with jealousy or shake his hand.

"Eddie said what?" There went the tea, and Owen was coughing, having choked on a breadcrumb or something.

"He said you and Joe would know what to get, and something about getting some good butt action."

"Damn." He laughed. Not at me, just into his hands. "I've always said Eddie bottoms."

"Does it matter?" I was so clueless about these things.

"No, of course not."

"Do you?" I had to swallow. "Bottom?" I had to ask. Because. You know? Essential information. It was slightly embarrassing how much I still had to learn.

He smiled and stirred the milk into his tea. There was a definite blush on his cheeks. "No. Not really. I only ever top these days."

"Oh."

"But that doesn't mean I wouldn't let you...you know...do me."

"You would?"

"Topping or bottoming, however you describe it, everyone should try both, at least once. It's not for everyone, and you might turn around and say, hey, Owen. This bottoming thing is not for me. I would totally respect that by the way. There are a million different ways to have sex. Whatever floats your boat, we can work with."

"I like that we can talk about this," I mumbled, but I did because it helped. Made me feel less anxious about it. I grinned. "I'd totally want to do you, but I need help."

"No, you don't. Just do what feels good. We're going to have a lot of fun figuring this out. Just...kind of try things." He became quiet, taking a careful sip of his tea. "You know, babes. I really—and I mean that—*really* love that we can talk about these things too. It's good that we can lay things on the table. Talk about how we feel. It's important."

"Yeah." I was off in dreamland too. Staring at him. It wasn't just my imagination. He had a definite semi brewing.

"So what did Eddie mean about toys?"

"I don't think he meant trucks and videogames."

I know that, Owen. He put his tea down.

"You're doing that thing again," I commented. Which he was. Any moment now, he would jump me because that was what he did. He'd go all bear on me, and I'd get to have another of those nice orgasms. I was starting to look forward to those. More than I wanted to admit.

"Hang on," I said, grabbing his wrists. Leading him over to the sofa, I gave him a little push so he got his arse down. He seemed to know what I meant, shuffling his hips over and leaning back as I awkwardly stood between his knees.

"You're not allowed to look. And don't laugh."

"Would I ever?" he asked, sounding a little faint.

"You would." I took to my knees, feeling a right prat. This was so out of my comfort zone that it wasn't even funny. But then this was Owen, and I was a little high on caffeine and feelings.

I leant down and moved my head from side to side so that his now kind of hard dick stroked my cheek. All those smells of him were so much stronger down here, like the concentrated version. *Eau de Owen*. I needed to get that bottled, keep some handy in my pocket for the next time life hit me in the face.

Not that I needed it now, with my nose buried in his pubes and my lips at the root of his dick. A small groan came from up above.

"Don't look," I reminded him.

"Not looking."

It took a little pep talk with myself, a deep breath and a whole lot of bravery, but I opened my mouth and slid the tip of his dick inside.

Not easy. There was no way I'd be doing what he'd done to me. I could get the tip in, and I sucked tentatively as he made noises. Grunts. Then he grabbed my hand and folded my fingers around the root. Ah. Better. So a hand-mouth-combo. I could do that.

I knew what felt good. Slow, steady strokes, though I made some goddamn awful slurping noises. My mouth watered with the intrusion as I bobbed carefully up and down.

Not exactly expert-like, but I moved on to licking, wetting my palm and gently pulling at his foreskin as I continued to explore with my mouth. And it hit me with a flash, bringing another rush to my head. I could do this. I was actually enjoying this. I didn't even have a hard on, but I...

There it was. A moan. From me.

I was officially totally embarrassed.

"I'm...going... Ahhhhhr!"

That was Owen trying to speak, and me sucking dick.

"Did you say something?" I smiled up at him with his dick smearing wet stuff all over my chin.

"Tap you on the shoulder...means I'm about to bloody explode all over you."

"Fair warning." I sucked the head of his cock back in my mouth, humming a little as it went even further in than before. My jaw ached as I bobbed up and down and he shouted half words over my head. Then he was gripping my hair and his hand hit my shoulder, and I supposed that was the warning or something but...

I pulled off just as the first load hit the roof of my mouth.

Slight shock, because I hadn't expected that, despite his warning, but it was...a weird turn-on. Especially combined with him shouting "FUCK!" at the top of his voice and trying to pull my hair out of my head.

I was actually rather good at this, getting his dick back in my mouth in time to swallow down more of the salty warmth. It wasn't unpleasant. Just...weird. And I was horny, my dick now wanting to play, but I was struggling to coordinate my hands and my mouth, and my knees were singing with discomfort from the hardwood floor and there! Another squirt of white from his dick. I licked it off. Because...why not?

He roared, grabbed my shoulders and tried to get me up so he could kiss me, so I ended up splayed across him, having him maul my mouth as his hand jerked at my happy dick that was definitely up for playing along.

He groaned. "Fuck that was so good. I really want to make you come. How do you want it?"

"Is there a menu?" I piped up with a smile as he kneaded my bum cheek and his fingertip smoothed over my hole, pushing cheekily.

"Well," he grinned. "I'll need a few minutes to get back up if you want me to fuck you, but, I can give you a sneaky hand job? Blow job?"

"Hmm." I pretended to think about it. He just laughed and kissed me.

"Or..." he said tentatively. "If you let me grab the lube and a condom? I can just ride you. Like this."

He flipped me over, so I was flat on my back on the sofa, and straddled me.

"Not enough space," he said. "Hang on." And what did I say about muscles?

I screamed as he picked me up right off that sofa and threw me over his shoulder. It wasn't elegant, and there was more than a little huffing and puffing and laughter as he carried me to the bedroom, but in seconds, I was flat on my back again and he was there on top of me with a bottle of lube in his hand.

"You're gonna drop me doing shit like that, and then I'll break my neck."

"Never."

"Why do we need condoms?" He hadn't used one with me, so I was...well. Confused. I needed a talk with Eddie. Get some ideas. Get a clue because I clearly had none.

"It's good to be safe. But also, sex is messy, and lube and condoms kind of make things... It's up to you. I get tested when I've been with someone, and I haven't been with anyone since uni. I'm pretty sure we're safe. And you?"

"Virgin boy here has no idea." I grinned.

"Virgin boy, my arse. I'm pretty sure you were pretty well fucked last night. And if you're up for it, let me get that gorgeous dick of yours all dressed up and then we'll..."

He stopped and swallowed as he flicked the lube open because I was being that embarrassing person again, lying on my back stroking my dick like I knew what I was doing. I didn't, but it felt good, and the way he looked at me was doing things to my head again.

He shuffled down and drizzled lube all over his hand before reaching back and...

Oh. Oh. OK.

"Gimme the lube," I demanded reaching for it. He did, and I drizzled what was probably half the bottle into my hand before I coated my dick.

"Ohhh."

Yeah. Lube. My new best friend. Nice. Now I was humping my hand, and Owen's mouth was open and his fingers were no doubt up his arse, and this was probably the most weirded out I'd ever been, yet in my head, I was suddenly some kind of king of sex and my brain felt like cotton. I was...I was going to...

"Don't come yet." He tugged my hand away from my needy dick and walked over on his knees.

Close. Too close. And now I was pinned down with him on top of me, and my hips were trying to hump whatever was there, and then he kissed me and I had to bite my bottom lip not to come.

"Going...to ride you," he murmured. "You're going to fuck me...good."

OK.

I wasn't lying. I was green. Sooo bloody green because all I could do was throw my head back as my dick got manhandled up his arse. There was no flowery prose in my head to describe it. Just raw. Sweaty. Bloody lube. More lube. Fingers digging into his hips as he pushed himself down, then stilling as his breaths hit my face. My legs cramping with my heels digging hard into the mattress.

Close. He was so close. And I was inside of him, and I didn't even know how to make sense of that. Just his lips on mine, and his tongue in my mouth and his arse in my palms, and then he started to move, and I think I shouted. I may even have screamed at one point, urging him on. *More. Faster. Do it. Keep going. Fuck, Owen, faster!*

We both seemed to come to our senses a while later, the two of us lying on our backs with our limbs splayed out like starfish on top of the covers, his breathing now calm, my fingers searching for his. Orgasms. Sex. Best. Shit. Ever.

"So, babes. Do you think this means we're verse?" he asked with a smile. I could hear it in his voice.

"What does that mean?" I was smiling too and didn't care what it meant as long as I could lie here all exhausted and sated. I did actually know what it meant. Go me.

"That we like having sex with each other, however that looks. We both top and both bottom."

"You said you didn't like bottoming."

"Yeah." He turned over to face me. "I never really have, but I liked what we just did. That was good stuff."

"Good stuff," I laughed. "I think I'm going to have to replace the vodka with this kind of good stuff."

"No, sweetheart. We're going to ditch the vodka. You don't need it now you have me."

"So I'm going to replace the vodka with...you."

"Yeah. Good plan. Whenever you think you need a drink, you remember that you have me, and that I will always be here to look after you, OK?"

His fingers stroked my hair, picked a strand out of my eyes. My fingers landed on his arm, drawing lazy lines over his wrist.

"So...we're going to this wedding tomorrow."

I was deflecting. It was a little too much to take in. The feelings, life, the realisation of how much had changed. Too much or too little, everything was different now.

"Yup."

"I think...things will be OK in the end."

"They always will be. As long as we have each other."

I nodded. Grinned like the idiot I was. I didn't believe in fairy tales, but somehow, this kind of felt like one. A weird bullshit one, but fuck. If this was my happy ending, I would happily settle for being bloody Snow White. Cinderella. Whatever.

chapter nineteen

Owen

I felt like I'd run a marathon, and it wasn't because I'd worked more shifts or magically discovered running. No. I'd had more sex in the past twenty-four hours than ever before in my life. And the backs of my legs were on fire and my thighs hurt and we'd had a fit of giggles this morning over our sticky arseholes.

Then we had shower sex.

Ugh.

Best thing ever.

And I knew this wasn't a bloody fairy-tale. I could tell Harry still had wobbles. I still said words that triggered him into a mess. He doubted himself more than he needed too, but I got it. I did. I doubted myself too, and that lid from the vodka bottle still sat at the bottom of the recycling bin? Mocked me with fear every time I stood next to the sink.

I'd been a teenaged mess of angst once too, and it had taken years to figure myself out. To stand on my own two feet and own who I was. I did now. But Harry hadn't had my journey, and his was just starting and I was under no illusion that the year ahead would be filled with shitstorms and drama. Worries. Doubts. Incidents where we would argue. Where I would lose my calm and he would drown himself in whatever he could find. He was my...man. And I had no idea how to save him.

Yet, I thought that, stood here puffing my chest out in a suit that probably cost more than my monthly wage, but I looked good. Damn, I looked good. Almost as good as Harry who I could tell had been tailored within an inch of his life into that suit. Brian was obviously skilled at what he did. And Harry swung around letting that jacket hug his hips and show off the arse on him and I was licking my lips and wondering if it would be form for the two best men to disappear off into the men's room before the service. For some...yeah. No.

But we were early, stood in the grand entrance to the venue. I'd had doubts when Joe had first told me where they had booked to get married, but standing here, I had to kind of agree with their choice. The place looked amazing. A grand old townhouse converted into a restaurant slash wedding venue. A small courtyard garden covered in roses that was bathing in the early morning sun. Champagne glasses carefully placed on a table in the middle, ready to be filled. It was smart. Classy, and the dining room set up was even more grand, yet surprisingly intimate. Blindingly screaming wedding. All whites and creams and dashes of silver running across the elaborately set tables.

And what made it even better was the nervous grin on Harry's face as Joe's mum made a beeline across the room, a terrified look on her face.

"Harry!" She huffed. "Thank God you're here, I need your help. The flowers are all wrong, there is no symmetry between the tables."

"It looks amazing," Harry politely replied, his hand searching for mine. "I'm sure it's something we can easily fix."

"You have a good eye, I mean, you're the one who noticed the frosting on the top tier of the cake would clash with the ribbons. I hadn't even thought of that, and I am. Grateful." Jane was almost calm. Almost.

"Show me these flowers," Harry said in a low voice. Like he was in control. I liked when this side of him came out. Work-Harry. The professional side of him. And my heart ached a little because I loved my Harry. The stupid playful slightly...hilarious man who I still struggled to believe...was...with me. Mine. I didn't dare to admit it to myself, still half expecting us to inevitably crash and burn.

Harry was far too handsome for me, and somewhere in the back of my head I feared he would discover that sex was great and go looking for it with other men. Better looking men. Richer men. Men with better skills than my pathetic Grindr experiences.

And now he was waltzing off with Joe's mum, who was waving her arms around pointing out some invisible symmetry issues that I could neither make heads nor tails of.

"Oh, she found him."

Eddie. Thank God for that. Rescuing me from my thoughts of doom.

"Yeah?"

"She's been in a right panic this morning, even asked for Harry's number because apparently he has some kind of magic eye for colour schemes. God knows what she's on about but suddenly Harry is her new favourite person. Joe was in fits."

"You spent the night before your wedding together? Isn't that supposed to doom your marriage or something?"

Could have been a bad joke, but Eddie just laughed.

"We don't follow the rules. Ever. This wedding will be exactly what we want. Which is why we vetoed the band and the disco and all that crap. I am not dancing in public."

"You do realise that Jane has a band booked for later. And that there will be a dance floor?" I cringed. Well. Pretend cringed.

He just shook his head.

"I'm not dancing. Neither is Joe. But fuck it. As long as people have a good time I truly don't give a rat's arse."

"Edward!" I grinned.

He just grinned back.

"So, Harry," he started. "Things OK?"

I could tell there were nerves there. His hands were fiddling with his suit. Eddie had scrubbed up well. The fabric clinging to his body in all the right places. A huge white flower on his lapel. Pink tie, to match Joe's suit. A light grey three piece that would look bloody brilliant in those photos that would no doubt hang on their wall for the rest of their lives. He looked fabulous. His arms bulged in that nice way. Not that I wanted to lick them. Not really.

"Things are good. One day at a time."

"And...you're getting on all right?"

Just shoot me now. I knew exactly what he was hinting at. And so did he, blushing beautifully under that fringe of his.

"I know you gave him sex advice." I hummed under my breath.

"I've been dying to give him the talk," he replied in a voice that felt slightly strained.

"So you knew?" We were both speaking in riddles here. Trying to be subtle. Respectful. Not say too much.

"Look," he coughed nervously. "I've known Harry all my life. There are a lot of things I know that I would never share. Trust me. But there are also things you need to understand. His...homelife...was...it shaped him. It was not like he turned up at school covered in bruises or anything, but there were things going on that no kid should have had to go through. There was this one time, we were probably around...seventeen? I'd just come out, and was trying to deal with being me and navigating this whole thing with Joe, and we turned up at Harry's house to pick up his kit and his dad was there and his dad just looked at me in disgust. Pure hatred. Then he said something about me being a raging homosexual and that he hoped it wouldn't rub off. Something like that. And Harry flinched like his dad had just punched him in the face. It was one of those moments where everything just fell into place for me. Where things made sense and all I wanted to do was to take Harry out of there and take him home and let my mum talk some sense into him. When I came out, back then, Mum gave me a stern talking to and told me never ever to hold anything like that back. That she was so bloody proud of me, proud of who I was and...and for...for loving Joe. And I wanted someone to tell Harry that his dad was wrong. I think I did actually, it's a little vague now because...it was one of those defining moments. Where I promised myself to get better at standing up for myself. Where I knew I could make a choice. I could be with Joe and be happy, or I could go back to being scared. I didn't want to be scared. I didn't want to ever feel like I did that day, again. I didn't want anyone to have to be Harry in that moment. I didn't even feel sorry for myself. I was just devastated for him, having to hear that from his own dad."

"Thanks...for looking after him."

"Thanks, yourself."

The air was thick and there was something in my eye. And Eddie was rocking his heels and I could tell he needed to speak. That there were a million things he'd probably bottled up that would one day have to be shared.

No kid should have to grow up like that. And I was suddenly incredibly grateful to have someone like Eddie in my life. In Joe's life. In Harry's life.

"So..." I was trying to choose my words carefully. "Harry said you had talked about...toys."

The grin on Eddie's face was hysterical.

"Please tell me you need me to send you some links. No, don't even tell me, because I will send them anyway. I know Joe will never share these things, but there are some...ahem...tried and tested items that I would be delighted to...recommend."

"Eddie. You are quite the dark horse."

"Not really. Joe does all the research. I'm just happy to be the guinea pig and try things out. Some things are truly not fit for purpose. Others may look innocent and lame, but..." He giggled. "As I said. Harry is all new to this. I don't want to overwhelm him by buying him a Prostate King XL for his birthday, even though I've been dying to."

"Eddie." I groaned.

"I really like the Njoy pure plugs too. The reviews are mixed but it's one..." He stopped and smiled as I hid behind my hands. "Too much? Let me send you that link."

"Yeah. Send me a link."

"I will do." He smiled. Laughing at me as I tried to gather myself back up. "Have you written a speech?"

"Yeah. Kind of."

"And Harry? I told him not to worry. It will be enough for him just to have to get through the day."

"He is doing well."

"Don't for a minute think he'll do this the easy way. He can be sneaky and hard work. But you know that."

"I have no illusions that we will skip off into the sunset," I agreed. "We'll figure it out as we go."

"Good plan. I will be here, should you ever need me. I've said for years that he should be in some kind of therapy, but he won't. So we will just have to keep him afloat. And I think...Joe's mum has got a thing for him."

He nudged over towards the head table where Harry now was picking flowers out of some kind of over-the-top arrangement as Jane was clapping her hands.

"She's a funny lady."

"She has her moments. Thing is. She's Joe's mum. And he's Joe. And they just have their thing where they have to fight over everything. He's good at standing up to her now, and I like that. I think she likes that too. Thrives on it. Pushing him to argue his case."

"He's bloody brilliant, Joe."

There was something in my eye again. I was not going to cry today, I'd promised myself.

"I'm going to walk down that aisle and marry my Joe and then we are going to go and be happy. That is my plan for the day. Nothing more nothing less. All this fluff and cake and stuff is just background noise. It really doesn't matter, but that is what Jane wants and Joe is happy and..."

"You've got something in your eye."

"Shut up, Owen."

"I'm glad...that the two of you are in my life."

I was a sap. Harry was right. I couldn't stop smiling.

"Ditto, mate."

He was dabbing his eye with a scrunched-up tissue. God help us today. There would be tears. At least I was prepared, grabbing a fresh packet out of my pocket and carefully handing him one. He blew his nose. Huffed. Shook his shoulders like he was trying to get himself together.

"Go rescue Harry, she has him sorting out the curtains now! He'll need a drink if we let her go on."

"He'll be fine," I promised. He would be.

"Go marry your boy." I slapped Eddie's back. Gave him an awkward man hug.

"Go marry yours. I'm counting on having to drag Harry through all this in the near future. He better ask me to be his best man, otherwise I will sulk."

I didn't even respond to that. Just smiled as I made my way through the sea of glittery napkins and flowers and fairy dust.

I agreed with Eddie. It was just background noise, but I would have lied if I didn't think it was beautiful. Because it was, and Harry was smiling, standing in the middle of it all.

chapter twenty

Harry

"I do," Eddie blurted, bawling his eyes out. His suit was crumpled at the front where Joe's hand had fisted his lapel, holding on to him like he would fall off the podium if he didn't.

"I do too," Joe said, grinning and trying to wipe Eddie's face dry with his sleeve.

I was pretty sure that hadn't been the order of the day, and the officiant looked slightly bemused. The two of them had apparently written vows, but I had no doubt those had gone out the window with all the crying.

Joe's pink suit was perfect. His glittery Converse, slightly insane. But that was who he was, and I was strangely proud of him for being exactly who he was. And Eddie? Yeah. He was Eddie. His jacket clung to those huge, sculpted arms like it had been sprayed on, and he was sobbing like a baby. Over-emotional—he'd always been that way, even back at school. He'd cried when we'd lost at rugby, cried every time he passed a test, and he had no shame. If it had been Owen and me up there, I'd have been in floods of tears too—and hiding in the loos. That beach wedding seemed ideal…if I ever got married. I wasn't sure I could ever do this. Well. Maybe. It was funny how these thoughts were rumbling around in my head.

There wasn't a dry eye in the house, and where once I would have found this more than cringeworthy, today, I had a lump in my throat. I distracted myself by watching Joe, who was laughing and trying to get Eddie to blow his nose, and then everyone was taking photos and cheering. The noise was enough to completely drown out the officiant, who must've told them to kiss, as the two of them were eating each other's snotty face.

Slightly unsavoury if you'd asked me, but I was cheering along, and then Owen grabbed me and kissed me and things just. Were.

As the confetti rained down, I realised Jane had been right. It was bloody perfect. Who would have thought that tiny pieces of paper sprinkling through the air like snowflakes would make me sob like a baby? The first time Eddie and Joe had kissed, it had randomly snowed. There'd even been an old, crumpled photo of the special moment—I knew because Eddie had spent years with that photo as the background screen on his phone—but the snowflake confetti had been Eddie's mum's idea. Apparently, it was the only thing she and Jane had agreed on.

So now it was May, the room was filled with snowflakes, and there was some romantic slushy boy band song playing. Eddie and Joe hadn't known a thing about this part of the ceremony, and their faces were frankly embarrassing. But I supposed that was weddings. A massive cringe fest of feelings, and somehow I was joining in and...maybe even enjoying it? Laughing and cheering as Eddie and Joe walked down the aisle, holding hands, looking like...well. The only thing I could think of was that their future looked so bright they should have worn shades. Which made me smile even harder.

I'd been to weddings before, so I knew the drill. I shook hands when prompted, smiled politely, drank all the water in the bottles that kept appearing by my side, hid in the stairwell for a minute when things got too much... Drank another bottle of water. Breathed.

"Oh, dear child!"

"Maggie!" The last person I'd expected to see here.

"I was hoping I'd get to speak to you." She gave me a kiss on the cheek.

"You look amazing!" I gushed, and she did, all dressed up. I'd only ever seen her in her cleaner's overalls. "I didn't realise you knew Joe and Eddie." Why did I not know? What the fuck?

She smiled and cupped her hands around my face. "It's a small town, child. We all know each other, one way or another. You look healthy. Good for you. No more of those nasty bruises, I see?"

"Nope." What could I say?

"I'm Jane's great-aunt, incidentally. I've known Joe since he was a scrawny little kid. Just like you. Not so scrawny now, the two of you."

I grinned. Surreal? Yes. Very.

"Now, did you, by any chance, find the coffee machine?" she asked.

"What?"

"I went to water those poor plants only to find they'd all been left in that terrible skip. I took them back inside and spruced them up a bit. Took me a few rounds to bring them home, one by one. They were fine inside. There was no need to throw perfectly good plants away like that. And they'd put your fancy coffee machine in that skip too, so I rescued it in case you came back. I know how much you liked that silly thing. I was never one for the coffee. Good strong cup of tea for me."

I was almost in tears again. I grabbed her hands and held on tight. "Thank you," I whispered.

"I was hoping you'd found it. Popped in on Thursday and everything was gone. You can have the rest of the plants back too if you want. I didn't want them to die." She looked guilty like she'd taken something she couldn't.

"Those plants were the only good thing in that place," I said softly. "I'm glad you have them. That makes me happy. And thank you for rescuing my coffee machine."

"It made me ever so upset. After all that rubbish those men put you though, demanding this and demanding that, and they didn't even bother to take it all away. They just threw it out. Lazy gits." She shook her head. "But never mind. The only thing that matters is that you are fine, child. You're looking well."

"I am well," I said.

She nodded and smiled. "Did you know your father and I went to school together?" She laughed. "He was always the same."

She looked at me, really looked, and there was a sense of warmth that I hadn't felt in a while.

"You were never like him. Remember that. You tried so hard to please him, but it was never you. You had your moments, I'll give you that, but you're not like him, Harry. You never were."

"I know." I hadn't thought about it. Not for days. But it felt good to hear someone say it. It was nice to feel...I was trying to think of the right words. Bloody words. Seen? Yeah. It was nice to have been seen. I didn't know how to tell Maggie, but somehow I thought she understood.

"I need to go find my sister. She gets very nervous on her own. I look forward to having a little dance later—if you fancy coming and swinging old Maggie around the dance floor?"

"I'd like that." I couldn't dance, but I doubted it would matter.

"Thank you." She tapped me on the shoulder, gave me another tap on my cheek. "Talk to that plant of yours. Tell it all your worries. Plants always listen. And give it a little squirt of water. They like that. Not too much. Just enough to keep it happy. Remember that. You never need too much. Just enough to keep you happy. And then a little bit more."

I didn't know if she'd read my mind, but I got it. I did. She hugged me again before patting me on the cheek. Again. It was what she'd always done.

"Maggie?" I started but couldn't find the words I should perhaps have said.

"I know," she said softly. "I know, child. You're happier now. That's all that matters." Then she walked off and left me standing, dazzled, in the sunshine streaming through the still-open door.

I *was* happier.

I held on to her words as the day went on. Things were easier now, and I managed. Step by step. Minute by minute. I held on to Owen when I wobbled, and I smiled every time I remembered he was mine, that I didn't have to question it. He was mine, and I was his. And maybe I was even doing a good job of looking after him. At least a little?

Still, I felt stupid, everyone keeping an eye on me, but at the same time, it felt safe knowing if I fucked up, someone would catch me and sort me out before I even got that drink down my neck. Which weirded me out no end.

The food was delicious, and the caterers were on the ball, topping up my glass of lemonade without me having to ask. I even had a slice of lemon in it like a grown-up, but I might as well have been sitting at the kids' table.

As dessert hit the plate in front of me, my gut started to churn, knowing the speeches were next. I ate slowly, wondering if I could do it. Stand up and speak without having a total panic attack. This wasn't some stupid bankruptcy meeting that would always end the same way. It wasn't a client meeting. No overdressed bank employee demanding I pay them back all the imaginary money I'd never even had in the first place. I'd dealt with those and survived. This, with everyone I had left in the world in the same room...

The expectations were crippling me, and for the first time, I considered pretending to go to the toilet and necking some leftover champagne to calm my nerves. I wanted to. Badly. But then Owen's hand was in mine, and I was squeezing his fingers too hard.

"You'll be fine, babes," he whispered. "You don't have to do this."

And then the video camera right in my face with Kim behind it, his eyes scrunched up in concentration as he carefully zoomed past Owen shoving a spoonful of chocolate mousse in my gob, feeding me like a baby.

"Joe's dad will announce me first," I said once Kim had moved on. "It's not like I can't say anything."

"You just stand up and say, 'To the happy couple! Cheers!' Done. Dusted. Easy."

"That's cheating." My heart was already racing, and I shouldn't have drunk two pints of lemonade because now I needed to go pee. For real.

"Only do what you can cope with," Owen stage-whispered as the camera once again swept past us. "Nobody expects an Oscar-worthy performance, not even our friend Kim and his camera here."

It was time.

Joe's dad looked as uncomfortable as I felt, announcing that the first speech would be... Me.

I stood up as if in a trance, almost tipping my chair over as I fumbled in my pockets for the stupid notes I'd made earlier. My mind was blank. Totally. And my ears were full of static, but people had...expectations.

I sat down. Then somehow stood up again with Maggie's words still ringing in my ears. *I'm not like him. I'm happier now.*

"Hi," I said weakly. "I'm Harry. For those who know me? Yeah. I don't know why Eddie chose me for this gig either."

Nervous laughter. Shit. Kill me now.

"For those who *don't* know me, I'm the guy who used to play naked in Eddie's paddling pool. And he once took a dump in mine."

More laughter. *Fuck you, Harry. Fuck you. Fuck EVERYTHING.*

"But that's not why I'm here today. I'm not here to tell you stupid jokes or embarrass myself more than I have to."

I had to take a deep breath and felt Owen's hand carefully stroke my back.

Another deep breath.

"I'm here because Eddie once told me a story about friendship, and I'm not talking about casual mates or the people you once went to school with. Not even those distant family members you might see once a year. Those are all important people in our lives, and no disrespect to anyone sitting here thinking they're Eddie's and Joe's friends. We all are. Otherwise, we wouldn't be here."

Owen's hand was still there, making slow steady strokes, bringing down my heart rate a little bit at a time.

"There are some friends who you spend your whole life thinking you don't deserve. The people who are simply there, through the good times and through the bad. Not many people stick around through the bad days. When you feel like you're trudging through mud and it never stops raining. And I think, what I am trying to say is..."

Stupid words. I was making no sense.

Another breath.

"Sometimes, those muddy patches turn out to be where things start to grow. Where the people who have always been there start to truly become your friends and friendships grow into something else. And I think that happens to most of us. Sometimes totally out of the blue. Other times, you know it's there, and it pulls at you, grates down all your defences until it's perfectly clear that some people...are just meant to be..."

Hums. Yeah.

"Even if you're not gay."

I had to say it, and laughter spread gently through the room. I laughed too.

"I used to say that, all the time. I wasn't gay. By the way, this is Owen. My partner. He's a bloke. I think I'm kind of gay. Funny how things turn out, eh?"

It was freeing to be able to say it out loud and see how people's faces were all smiling and kind, their laughter not mocking but trickling through the air like little shiny raindrops.

"The truth is, I'm here because I grew up with Eddie, and because he trudged through the mud with me when I couldn't even start to dig myself out. Then he met Joe, and yeah, you all know that story. But Eddie was still there for me. And then Joe... Well, this isn't just a story about Eddie because without the two of them, I wouldn't be stood here making the world's most disorganised best-man speech."

More laughter. Thank God. I needed to breathe. Drink. Not pass out.

"What I want to say is, without the people in our life who hold us together, we wouldn't last very long. And all the people who have held me together over the past years are in this room. You know who you are."

Fuck. If I didn't stop now I would start to cry. I looked at Eddie. Joe. People from school. Familiar faces. Unfamiliar ones too. Maggie nodding supportively from the corner table.

"Back to the mud. Out of that mud grows friendships, life, new beginnings. And that is what I want to say. This is a wedding, but it's not the end of the romance. It's not the end of anything. This is the start of some amazing new things for Eddie and Joe. There will be new things for them to grow. New experiences. New people. Married life. Going on their honeymoon. Oh wait..."

The room exploded with laughter. I grinned.

"Eventually."

More laughter. I was strangely enjoying this.

"Eddie will never again forget to book his annual leave, and Joe will one day forgive him."

Yup.

"There's a whole life ahead for Eddie and Joe. And guys?"

I tried to look at them, but the lump in my throat wouldn't let me, so I looked at my hands. Tried to breathe.

"Guys, just make it count. Make every bloody day count. Don't let things...things that are unimportant take over. Nothing in the world should be more important than what the two of you have. You have each other, and that is just...insanely cool. There's been a whole eight years of Eddie and Joe already. And I feel very, *very* privileged to have been allowed to tag along for the ride. The ups, the downs, the happy times and the times when I unfortunately behaved like some deranged arsehole."

It was true. And there were nods out there in the crowd, blending into the laughter. I didn't mind.

"Today, we start at ground zero. The first day of a brilliant future. A future so bright..." I got my shades out of my pocket, put them on like a twat. People howled with laughter, and I nodded. Like a fool.

"But seriously. I love you guys. Eddie, thank you. For every time when I didn't say thank you. Joe, thank you for not strangling me in my sleep. I wouldn't have blamed you. Not one bit. And honestly? I wish you every happiness in the world. I can't wait to see what the future holds. To Eddie and Joe!"

"To Eddie and Joe!" echoed through the room as glasses were held up and I slumped back on my chair. I hadn't planned on saying any of that, but at least I'd remembered the

shades, thinking I could get that phrase in somewhere. Eddie would get it. We'd always done it as kids. Put our shades on thinking we were cool. *Our future's so bright, we have to wear shades.*

Owen pulled them off me and planted his lips on mine. Snogged the life out of me, both of us grinning like fools.

"Damn it, babes. Now my speech will be all lame."

"It will be brilliant," I whispered. I was drained, exhausted, and shoved the last of my chocolate mousse into my mouth, downing it with the last dregs of flat lemonade.

Then Eddie was there dragging me up on my feet and hugging the shit out of me with his face in my neck. There were bloody tears, and I hated that, I did. I sobbed like a baby. But Eddie was there. And Owen. And Joe. And I was crying and smiling and the sun was shining, and suddenly I couldn't even remember what the tears were for.

chapter twenty one

Owen

"To Eddie and Joe!"

I raised my glass, cheering as Joe's dad sat himself back down. Another speech done and dusted. I still had the lump-of-doom in my stomach hearing all the reminiscences and funny stories. Most of them I knew. Others had slightly rocked me. I would forever be grateful to the universe for letting me have an easy ride. Life had thrown me hurdles, but compared to others, I was fine. More than bloody fine.

"I'm not dancing later. Just sayin'." Joe leaned against the table, watching the event staff carrying in equipment and speakers and what looked like a DJ set-up with a neon light ramp. "But I've snuck in a box of board games, and Eddie's mum is setting up a games table in the conservatory for later. So when everyone else is dancing, I'm going to force you to play a round of Lido with me, just like we used to do at uni, because it's my wedding and this is what I want. When everyone else was drunk and disorderly, you and I used to hide in my room and play games. Remember?"

I laughed. We'd been kids, really. "Honestly? If someone offered me a night out on the town, limo, free drinks all night, all the handsome naked men in the world begging for my attention, I'd still choose a game of Lido with you." I was serious.

Joe snorted. "Now you're being kind. You'd still want to ogle those naked men."

"Yeah, maybe. But only to look. I'm taken now." I brushed down my sleeves, awfully pleased with myself.

Joe rolled his eyes and sighed. "I can't believe you're banging Harry Thunder. Out of all the people in the world."

"Well. He is kind of special."

"That he is. I really enjoyed the day out Mum and I had with him, so I was thinking...I could take him somewhere next week. Mum wants to go to that big garden centre, you know? The one full of old ladies drinking tea and eating scones in the front? Not my scene, but..."

I nodded and smirked. It was one of Joe's favourite places, but not for the old ladies eating scones. Hidden at the back was a nerdy space with local art exhibitions and books and comfortable chairs and the best cake known to man.

"They're doing another freestyle art class," Joe continued. "And, I mean, even you liked it last time."

"I did." I'd been useless and still had paint on my best trainers, but it was another day out with Joe that would forever be part of my happy memories.

"Anyway, Mum's sudden crush on Harry is more than embarrassing. It's like she always needs a project, and now the wedding is over, she's set her sights on giving him a professional makeover, coaching his future career and sprucing up his CV. She was asking if he had a LinkedIn account because she couldn't find him."

"Well, maybe that's a good start?"

"He's not ready to meet that side of Mum. She'll completely break him, have him quivering under the table begging for mercy. You know what she's like."

I grimaced. "She'd have him CEO of some new start-up in no time." Somehow the thought of that seemed...wrong.

Joe took another sip of champagne, his hand in his pocket, looking more relaxed than I'd expected him to be today.

"You OK?" I asked quietly.

"I am," he replied. "I truly am. I'm now officially Joseph Tomlinson-Sumner. A proper adult married man. What the hell happened, Owen? These kinds of things don't happen to people like me."

"They do. They happen especially to people like you. Really good people with good hearts and kindness and...yeah. Good things happen to people like you, Joseph...Tomlinson-Sumner. Especially when you look as good as you do today. Even I would have flirted with you. You look hot, babes. Scorching."

He grinned. Then grimaced. We did that a lot.

"Promise me you won't tell any embarrassing stories from nursing college. I don't need the world to know that I fainted the first time I drew blood and that I should never be allowed to drink French brandy."

"Would I do that? And anyway, it wasn't *just* brandy. It was Eddie's mum's best cognac."

"Whatever it was, it was pure poison. And yes, you would. I want today to be happy. I don't want to remember the times when I didn't feel like I do today."

"I promise you." I took the champagne glass out of his hand and put it carefully on the table. Then I bear-hugged him until he squealed and kicked my shin so I had to put him down.

"Don't," he warned.

"My speech is lame," I whispered. "I'm basically just going to tell people how awesome you are. And that will be it."

"Good." He nodded nervously. Drained his champagne.

"Good," I agreed.

"Harry did well."

"He did."

"Are we back to two-word sentences?"

"Yup, babes."

"Good."

"Good."

"You see the guy in the green shirt over there? Blue tie?"

"Awful combo."

"Agreed. But he went to school with us, two years above. Total twat. Then he married Eddie's cousin, and hence he's here. I hated having to invite him, but he just came up and shook my hand. Said it was his first gay wedding and that he absolutely loved the whole set-up. They'd had a church wedding, apparently, it felt like a bloody funeral. Said he wished he'd worn a pink suit, and the guy was serious. Kind of made my day."

"Funny."

"Yeah. Funny how some people grow up to be decent. More than decent. What is it with school that makes everyone behave like bloody idiots? I mean, even you and me. Why the hell did we not get taught to stand up for ourselves? Why was everything always such a bloody drama? All the times I cried and hurt and thought the world was ending over small stupid things that didn't matter in the end. I can't even remember why that guy was a twat at school now. He just was."

"I know, babes. I know. People say that they would love to relive their teen years, but nope. Never in a million years."

"Hell, no."

Joe never swore. But he smiled, and I was again reminded of how lucky I was, how good my life was, simply because he was in it, riding this roller coaster with me.

"You look amazing, Joe."

"I know. I do, don't I?" He nodded before he got dragged away, leaving me standing there, wishing for all the good things.

So.

My turn, apparently, as people were slowly retaking their seats. I didn't take mine. Instead, I straightened my jacket and cleared my throat. Like a grown-up.

"Joe Tomlinson...Sumner. The man. The myth. The brilliant, totally grown-up husband looking rather radiant today."

People hummed in agreement.

Good.

I smiled. Because this was all ridiculous.

"I love that you are my best friend, babes. I love that we have ridden this rickety roller coaster together. The one called life—and the bit that's not life too. You know—that awkward stage where you leave school thinking you're an adult...and then life hits you in the face and you realise that you're anything but.

"I like to think I grew up with you, Joe, because the man you met on that first day of nursing college is not the man standing here today. You've been the most incredible friend. Not only have you taught me some amazing life lessons—thing that have shaped the man I've become—but you've also taught me about kindness. About love. About the absolute need for whipped cream in hot chocolate. The magic of a good pair of well-worn trainers.

You showed me how to apply glittery eyeshadow, which was one lesson I might not have fully taken onboard."

Laughter. I'd never wear make-up again. Not me. Ever.

"We did it because it was fun. I've always had fun with you. You told me about books to read. Songs I absolutely had to listen to. We went to see a play that broke my heart. Who knew a little backyard theatre could make me cry? You knew, so you took me to see it. And afterwards, we had our first ever tequila slammers. Life-changing memories that will always stay with me."

I wasn't crying. I was smiling, and so was Joe.

"Babes, I will round this up before Eddie starts to worry. Because I do love you. Your playlists are legendary. Your laughter, infectious. And the way you always win at Catan? I still suspect there are some sneaky tricks to winning that game that I have yet to learn from you, and I hope that you will keep on teaching me things. That you will be the one who'll always stand next to me when I need a helping hand. And that we will always be what we are now. The best of friends."

I raised my glass.

"Eddie. Look after your man because he's one in a million. And he may be wearing a pink suit, and he may kill me next...or even cheat the next time I agree to play Monopoly with him, but despite Joe once dropping a syringe that ended up stabbing me in the foot..."

I wasn't expecting laughter for that, but I got it.

"I was fine, by the way. And I don't blame him for the three months of blood tests and antibiotics that followed."

Joe was going to kill me. Well, he wouldn't, we'd always laughed about it. It would always be part of who we were.

"Joe is the strongest man I've ever known. The one who would plough down Roman armies to protect his friends. The one who would stand up to anyone who tried to do harm to the people he loves. He would slay anything that ever tried to come between him and Eddie. I know. I've played Dungeons and Dragons with these two, and you *do not want* to be on the other team. Top tip. Don't. You won't make it."

Truths right there.

"Joe, you've shown me what it's like to be strong. You showed me I could have that strength too. When I really wanted something, you were there pushing me to go and get it, and when I was going wrong in life, you'd gently steer me in the right direction."

Deep breath.

"And that's where I will leave you. With friends. Best friends. And the best people I know. My Joe and his Eddie. Cheers!"

I turned to grab Harry. I felt a little high, realising I'd pulled it off, and needed him to calm my racing heart, but my hands fumbled in thin air.

He was gone. Not next to me. Not in the room either, I realised, as I spun around, helplessly flailing my arms.

"Harry?" I called out. "Have you seen him?" I asked the people closest to me. They shook their heads and carried on celebrating.

I ran out in the courtyard, looking all around, my chest on fire with sudden nerves and anger. Where the hell was he? I'd kill him. Truly. If he was hiding somewhere downing whatever he'd found, I would bloody kill him. Not now. Not today. But he—

There he was, out in the entrance hallway. Walking towards me with his phone in his hand.

"OMG, babes, where have you been? I couldn't find you anywhere!"

He grimaced, rolling his eyes. I was officially annoying the crap out of him. He wasn't a child, and I wasn't his mother, but still. What the hell?

He looked grey again. Pale. Exhausted. Distraught. And then he laughed. A weird, cackling laugh like he couldn't even control it.

"I need to sit down. Fuck... Shit!" He crouched on his haunches, right there in the hallway, tugging at his hair. I grappled with him, getting him to stand back up so I could hold him, kiss his hair, remind him of everything that was good here.

"Talk, Harry. Words. Now."

Stern perhaps, but he needed to know I was not going to let anything go wrong today. Whatever he was up to needed to stop. Now.

He pushed me away, gently, wiped his face with his palm and took a deep breath.

"Talk," I repeated.

"I haven't been drinking," he said quietly. "Calm the fuck down."

"Good." My two-word vocabulary had shrunk to one because I couldn't handle this. Not today.

"I just took a call from Social Services. Some Child Protection manager." He snorted. Looked at me in disbelief. "They want to meet with me. And you. You'll have to come too. I'm not doing this without you."

"What on earth for?" I squealed. I was just as bad as him. What the almighty fuck? "Tell me you haven't been lying about your age or something. Please God..." My head was spinning with deranged thoughts.

He laughed and planted a kiss on my stupid face. "I have a little brother going into foster care, unless they can find blood relatives willing to take him on."

"Fuck," I said.

"They probably won't let me. Owen. I need help. I can't even—I need a job. How the hell am I going to get a job? He's five. A five-year-old kid, Owen? What the fucking hell?"

"Fuck," I said again.

Yeah.

Fuck indeed.

chapter twenty two

Harry

I'd gotten up far too early, my thoughts too messy to even try to go back to sleep. It had been another one of those days— the muddy, shitty kind when I couldn't get my head around things.

I had a little brother. Not brand-new information. I'd known. But the thought of taking care of him, of raising a kid who was probably as messed up as me?

Genetics. Unavoidable. The kid was raising hell before he'd even set foot in our house.

But it wasn't my house. I was just assuming that Owen wanted this too. I didn't even know if he did. Did he want kids? Owen would be a great dad and could probably raise ten of them in his sleep. I couldn't even tie my own shoelaces.

What the actual fuck?

I kept muttering those words under my breath. *What the actual fuck?*

I'd left Owen to sleep and pottered around in my bare feet until I couldn't stand the sound of my huffing and puffing, so I'd brushed down Owen's suit and repacked it in the suit carrier, carefully tucked the tie back in its box.

A month ago, I'd still been at the office dredging through paperwork, tearing my hair out at everything going to hell.

Then I'd thrown myself into a relationship.

Moved in with a guy.

Given a fucking speech.

Not drunk a drop since...Thursday. Or whatever.

I was adulting at speed, and I had no idea what I was doing.

I'd sat at the kitchen table and tried to read up on foster care, but my head had gone into some kind of nauseating spin, so here I was, walking into town with the suit and my card in my pocket, gearing myself up to have that talk with Brian.

It was the right thing to do.

Because I needed to fucking take control.

He gave me that smarmy grin as I walked through the door.

"Morning, Brian." It was better to start on a polite note than let him set the tone.

"Master Thunder," he said politely.

"Cut the crap." I was tired of all of this.

"Tell me," he said, leaning forward and resting his elbows on the counter. "Did that man of yours look a million pounds?"

"He did." I smiled. He had, and it had been worth whatever was to come.

"He's a very handsome man."

"I know." I didn't even question my own thoughts anymore, which I decided was a step in the right direction.

"Told you. And the wedding? All good?"

"Perfection." I wasn't going to get into a conversation here. Just be polite. Sort things. Move on.

"Morning, Brian!"

Shit. Here was Jane, looking like she'd had fifteen hours' sleep and not stayed up until three in the morning dancing. I knew she had because when I'd swung Maggie around the dance floor in the world's worst attempt at the waltz, Jane had still been there and it had been after two o'clock. Maggie had made me promise to take dance lessons one day. I'd vowed to never dance again, but that was after Eddie and Joe and Owen and me and a bunch of others had played a full round of cheats Monopoly and I'd scammed Eddie out of all his money before Kim had bankrupted me. I'd taken it well. Honestly. And then we'd smuggled half the wedding cake out into the garden and ate it lying on the grass, staring at the stars.

It had been a good day. A good night. Yet I still couldn't relax and remember that because...life.

Fuck.

"Jane, as beautiful as always."

"Not a social call, Brian, but Harry, I'm glad I caught you! I was going to call later. I need to talk to you."

"Jane, don't do this again."

"Do what, Brian?" Looking slightly miffed, Jane placed a large suit carrier on the counter and glanced at me. "Rental suits. The way forward. Practical and economical." She winked.

"Mast...Harry, last time Jane was here, she poached herself a client, right under my nose. It was most disturbing."

"Nonsense." Jane laughed. "Matthew Purskin was a former client of mine anyway, and he was selling that house well under market price. I couldn't just stand here and let him make the worst decision of his life."

"You're a tax law consultant, Jane."

"I'm also a qualified mortgage advisor and a certified life coach. I have a very successful financial advisor set-up, hence I am more than qualified to tell when someone is making a massive error of judgement."

Jane was also terrifying.

"That doesn't mean you can use my business premises as your personal office." Brian was smiling as he said it. This was apparently how these two operated. I took a small step backwards.

"Do you want a coffee, Harry? Since Jane is apparently about to sit you down and give you advice on your *massive errors of judgement*?" He winked, and I gave him a nod. Fuck knew what was happening right now.

"Make that two coffees, Brian, and if we could have a few minutes of privacy. Go get your Andrew out of bed because I need this month's expenses broken down."

"Coffee I can do, but the two of you *will* be spilling the tea. Since you're on my patch."

With a sigh, Jane grabbed my sleeve and led me over to the bay window with the table and chairs, where I sat, as directed, feeling...like a small child.

"I heard," she said. "And I don't think this is a bad idea, at all."

"What exactly did you hear?"

"Douglas...and we shouldn't speak ill of the dearly departed, but Harry, your father was a permanent disaster waiting to happen. Discretion wasn't his forte, and I never blamed Felicity for taking off the way she did. Just so we have the air clear here. I'm not taking anyone's side, but this was hardly unexpected."

"Douglas Thunder." Brian was back in full smarm mode, placing a tray of three elegant cups of coffee on the wooden table in front of us. "The gift that keeps on giving. What has he done to you now? The bastard."

"Privacy, Brian." Jane sat up straight.

Brian pulled up a chair, sat and crossed his arms.

"Slight issue with a child in need of a foster placement. Young Harry here is about to embark on the journey of parenthood."

"Interesting."

I was surprised. He didn't seem a bit shocked, unlike me, swallowing spit and trying to keep my legs from shaking.

"First of all, Harry, I'm not here to do anything but support you. I may not have dealt with this side of social services before, but I have dealt with many other aspects, and my contacts within that department are all solid people."

"OK?" I wasn't sure what else to say.

"Secondly, if you decide to take this on, which I assume, from what Joe told me, you are considering, then I think it may be a very good opportunity for you."

"I don't have a job." Suddenly I'd found my voice. "I don't have an income. I don't own anything to house this kid in. I don't have any savings or any ways to even start supporting another person. I read up this morning, and I'll need paperwork and approval and all the references. I'll need people to write personal statements, not to mention that I have a drink problem and should probably have been in therapy since I was born."

Brian's chest heaved with held-back laughter.

"I think you have a very good idea of who you are, young man."

"Rule one in changing your life. Turn this around. Look at the positives." Jane had fished out her laptop and was now furiously tapping away at her keyboard. "Just making notes here so we can make a comprehensive plan."

"What positives?"

"You are a proactive, bright human being with a stable relationship and a home."

"I've been with Owen for two weeks. I squat in his bed."

Now Brian was laughing out loud.

"That's not what I'm hearing. And not what will go down in my personal recommendation."

"Where do I even start getting a job?"

"I wish I could say that I had an easy fix to that one, but I don't. Not that you will have time for immediate employment. We need to get you enrolled in a foster carer program as soon as possible." Jane stopped and tapped the screen with her finger. "We could even expand on this. We need to discuss your career aspirations, see what you have in mind, but for now, to build a case on your suitability for this? Childcare is a very honourable vocation, Harry, and one I think you would excel at. You did work with Eddie at the Rugby-tots club, didn't you?"

"It was one summer." I sighed. This was crazy.

"Perfect. And you enjoyed it?"

I shrugged. I'd been seventeen and had spent four weeks of the summer holidays hanging out with Eddie. Of course I'd enjoyed it. "A few weeks making sure a bunch of toddlers didn't choke on their lunches while playing silly ball games doesn't give me the right to raise this kid. This is my brother. Genetics. He'll be as fucked up as I am."

"Positivity, Harry. Look at it this way. We know nothing about his situation or where he's come from, but you're in a fantastic position to make a real change here. To take control again, steer your life onto a path that will turn the past into something good."

"I'll write you a personal reference too," Brian said enthusiastically. "After all, I made your Christening outfit. Dressed you for years. That surely makes me qualified."

"You have several really good people who would write excellent references," Jane agreed. "Maggie worked with you for your entire career within Thunder and Lightning. She always spoke highly of you."

"She was the office cleaner," I said quietly.

"What difference does that make? She was a colleague with whom you interacted on a daily basis. That makes an excellent referee."

She pinned me down with another stare. "Don't think this will be easy. If you think the last year was hard, then we can forget about it and let the child go into the system. But if you want this, we'll both have to knuckle down and prepare for a fight because you'll be dissected, every aspect of your life picked apart, and you'll start to question everything—your relationship, your abilities, your sanity."

Jane wasn't making this sound like a good idea at all, and I was once again trying to sink through the chair.

"If you do this, and you *can* do this, I will be here supporting you, but you will be doing all the hard work. You'll need to have nerves of steel, both for yourself and for Owen, because I don't doubt for a second that that boy won't have your back too. I always said to Joe that Owen needed to be a father. He's a very nice young man."

"And a very handsome one." Brian took a sip of coffee and gave me a wink.

"When is your initial meeting?" Jane asked.

"Wednesday."

"Good. I need to go do some research. Ring my contacts. It's Sunday, which is unfortunate, but I'm pretty sure this woman in my yoga class is a foster carer, so I'll make a swift social call later. Keep your phone handy so I can reach you."

"And what do I do?" I felt lost. So bloody lost.

"You gear yourself up to fight. Get your house in order. I'll email you a list of actions, a CV template, and think about the future. Would marriage be on the cards? If the two of you were married, we would have a stronger foundation to build on."

"*Two weeks!*" I almost shouted. "I've been with Owen two weeks! What are you on about?"

"I married Andrew after four months," Brian piped up. "Met him in a club, took him home. He never left. Funny how these things turn out."

"I remember." Jane smiled. She rarely smiled. "How long has it been now?"

"Fourteen years." Brian looked odd. Like he was actually...being genuine. "Still can't get him out of my bed."

"He's a lucky man." Jane was tapping away at her laptop again.

"I'm the lucky one," Brian said.

"Which brings me to the cost of the rental suit," I said and sat up straight. Control. I was taking it.

"Absolutely not." Brian sat up even straighter, refusing to break eye contact.

"I'm not leaving owing you any money."

"You *will* owe me after I've written you a glowing reference, describing your life in fabulously crafted menswear." Brian laughed. "Until then, you owe me nothing apart from popping in when you're in town and updating me on the proceedings. I need to know what's going on, and when this is all over, you will invite me to meet this young charge of yours, and Andrew and I will be godparents."

"Brian..." I sighed.

"It's an option. All right?"

I laughed because it was ridiculous.

My phone was still pinging with incoming emails from Jane as I walked up the stairs to find Owen fighting with the coffee machine, steam hissing out all over the floor. He threw a tea towel at it in disgust.

"I took the rental suit back," I said before he went into a full meltdown. "I left you a note."

"I saw. Thank you." The machine pushed out another angry hiss of steam.

"I still need to buy a milk jug."

"I'm throwing this machine out the window. It truly hates me."

"No, it doesn't. I had a meeting with Jane."

"Gosh, you've been busy."

"I know. I don't know where to start."

"You are going to start right here," he said, walking over and embracing me the way only he could. His dressing gown cord dug into my stomach as he kissed my neck.

"What's right here?" I asked, my nose in his chest.

"Me and you, and I have a day off, so we're going to sit down and have some breakfast and chill. Then we're going to talk about what we do next, and everything, whatever you decide, will be fine. Because I love you, and as Joe would have said, this is our life and we're going to live it exactly as we want to. Doing what we want, not what other people tell us is the right thing to do. OK?"

"I just want us to be happy," I mumbled into his shoulder, pressing myself against him.

"I am happy, Harry. I'm really happy. Are you?"

"Yeah, I am." I leant back so I could look at him properly. At the kindness in his eyes. The little wrinkles as he smiled. All that messy beard. His lips that leant down to kiss me.

"A few weeks back, I felt that I was all alone. It's really frightening. I could have disappeared down a black hole, and nobody would have ever known what happened to me. Or that's how I felt. That black hole kept eating me up, and all I wanted was to not be so alone, I just wanted someone to pick me up and drag me out. Every night when I went to bed, I wished I was here instead. With you. It breaks you when you get into that state, when fear and loneliness eat you up on the inside. It..." I smiled, gave a stupid little laugh. "It drives you to drink."

"I can imagine."

"I don't want my little brother to be alone."

"He never will be."

"I don't even know his name."

"Does it matter? He's your little brother, and we'll look after him."

"Jane says it will take time. We need to get approved and go through training. There will be meetings and we need references and...and...we'll need a bigger house."

"Whoa." He grinned. "First things first. If needed, he'll have our bedroom, and you and I will sleep on the sofa. Or on the floor. Whatever. One thing at a time."

"I need—"

"A job. Don't stress. This is a huge thing to go through, but we'll figure it all out. Whatever we need to do, we will do."

"It's just a lot in my head now. Jane is quite..."

"Forceful. I know. Joe rang me. She already made a list of things we can do to up our case. Like..." He grinned again. "Get married. Eventually put your name on the mortgage."

"Then I'll scam you out of every penny and run off with Brian the tailor." I was kidding, and he knew it, mock pushing me around and walking me backwards over to the sofa.

"Not after the blowie I'm about to give you. Sit down. Get your pants off."

"And then?" I dragged my jeans and boxers down over my now happily jerking dick.

The fact that I was doing this still gave me a pang of anxiety. It was fine. Except it wasn't, but then it was because it made me laugh that I was sitting on the sofa stroking my dick and Owen had placed a sofa cushion on the floor. Cheating, if you asked me. He knelt on the cushion and opened his dressing gown so my legs were against his chest and his face was in my stomach, kissing little lines down to my groin, and...

I didn't think many coherent thoughts after that. Just hot, wet mouth and my dick going all the way down his throat.

Owen was good. Bloody hell. How lucky was I? My head bent back over the sofa cushion, my mouth urging him on, my fingers digging into his back, trying to get the damn dressing gown off. I liked his arms. His shoulders. The way his hair felt beneath my palms. The noises his mouth made when he let me go, twisted his tongue around the head of my dick and flicked it over the slit. Things that made me shuffle further down the sofa so I could get my legs around his back, jerking helplessly as he took me down again. Deep. Sucking warmth. Sounds. Wetness. Sloppy noises. Asking for more. Much, much more. All of it. Give it to me. Right now. Fuck. Fuck. FUCK.

I loved that he swallowed me down. Let me spill into his mouth. Over and over again. Deep, sated whines came out of my mouth as the cold air hit my exhausted length. Saliva dripped from his smiling mouth, and he wiped it away, then he kissed me. A long, deep kiss that kind of took my breath away.

"I'd marry you tomorrow. You know that, right? I'm not here for fun. I'm here because you and me?"

"Yeah?" I asked hazily. I couldn't even think. My head was spinning again. With feelings. Happiness. Tears. Bloody tears.

"I want this, you and me. And your little brother—we will be a family. Imagine that. We will have good times, and there will be bad times, but we'll get through them because have I ever given up on you?"

"No."

"I fell in love with you the first time I saw you. Then you cheated at Monopoly, and you knew that I knew. You were smiling, and I felt faint. Stupid. I know. But sometimes being exactly who you are is why people fall in love with you."

"And who was I?"

"You were a right little shit. Joe was so annoyed with you."

"I remember."

"Then you got drunk and fell out the front door."

"Mmm."

"That was the first time you slept in my bed. I slept on the sofa."

"Disappointing." I was kidding. "I think I'd have had a heart attack if you'd tried anything. I wasn't ready for that. Not then. But I liked you. I really liked you. And you were Joe's friend, and I wanted you to look after me the way you looked after him. You adore him, and I wanted to be adored too. By you."

"I do adore you."

I grinned. "Thank you," I said. It felt weak. Stupid. But right. "If you…one day…want to marry me?" I was blushing but laughing at the same time. This was ridiculous.

"Are you proposing? I'm not even wearing pants. Come on, babes!"

"Go get some pants on then! It's a one-time offer!"

"Or maybe you're the one wearing too many clothes?" He gestured to my half-dressed self. I ripped the hoodie over my head. Got rid of my T-shirt. Kicked my trousers down, which didn't work. So Owen had to grab my socks, dragging them off my feet, followed by the trousers. My boxers went flying across the room.

"Sit down," I demanded. I could be bossy too. Take control. Be in charge.

He did. Smiling. "Now what, babes?"

I straddled him. His warm naked body under mine. Sat my arse on his lap and put my arms around his neck. "This... A lot has happened lately."

"It's been a ride," he said quietly. "I wouldn't change a thing."

"Neither would I. Well... Maybe more words. Less...vodka."

"We don't need the vodka."

"No."

I stroked his cheek with my fingertips, warmth spreading over my chest. I'd never wanted this. I'd spent my entire life fearing this. Intimacy. Love. Relationships.

Sex.

Dirty sexy stupid stuff. Things that people hid on their phones. Dodgy websites. Body fluids. Weird stuff.

Funny how things change.

"I want...to do things with you. And not just the...naked stuff. I heard your speech yesterday, before my phone rang and I had to run off."

"It scared me."

"Sorry."

"I want you in my life, however that will pan out."

"I want us. Like this. You and me. And I want to...Owen?"

"Yeah?"

"Wanna marry me? Just you and me, and we'll go down to the registry office or something, and then we'll go and have roast dinner with your mum. You keep saying we need to go see your mum for roast dinner. I want that."

"That sounds amazing." There were tears in his eyes.

"I don't want the big wedding. I don't want all the things like yesterday."

"Background noise. That was what Eddie called it."

"Background noise. I think we should just have the main event. You and me. You want a ring?"

"Nah. Just a kiss. And can I wear that suit again?"

"I'll ask Brian. I'm sure he'd be thrilled."

"Then we'll have roast dinner with Mum."

"OK. And have my little brother there."

"We can do that."

"Deal?"

"Deal."

"Harry?"

"Yeah?"

"Fucking love you."

I laughed. It was such a strange thing coming out of his mouth. Familiar. Safe. Warm.

"I love you too. Now get off the sofa and make me a coffee. I have an inbox full of things I need to do today, and then..."

"You owe me a blow job."

"Coffee first. And toast. I haven't eaten since yesterday, and now I'm starving."

I was happier now. And the sun was shining. I wrapped Owen's dressing gown around my naked body as he walked into the kitchen, naked, and once again swore at the coffee machine.

"Now the bloody thing's leaked water everywhere. I fucking hate this machine."

"No, you don't," I said with a grin.

I was happier now. I truly was.

chapter twenty three

Owen

ne year later

"Harreeeey!"

I could hear Luca's voice, and I hadn't even put my key in the lock yet. And when I did, he was shouting again.

"Haaarrreeeeeeeyyyyy!"

"Go find Daddy. He's just walked through the door. Go ask him."

"Daddeeeeyyyyy!"

Here he was. Luca. Just turned six. Bombing down the stairs at a speed that I still feared would make him fall over and break his neck. Also, I was Daddy. Harry was Harry. Everything we had learnt from our foster-care course thrown straight out the window because that was what Luca had decided we were to be called. He wanted a daddy. I was apparently it. And Harry had grinned and whispered, "Hey, Daddy," in that tone of voice that was simply irresistible. I'd threatened to spank him if he called me that again. He'd threatened to tie me to the bedposts if I did. We didn't have any bedposts. We were both safer that way, and anyway, we were parents now. Well...in a way.

"Luca, walk down the stairs. No running. We don't want to have an accident."

"But I want a new baby!"

OK.

This was apparently parenting. The constant random demands, never-ending questioning and a full-on life of chaos from seven in the morning until eight at night when Luca passed out in his bed, usually followed by me passing out on the floor next to him and Harry having to come drag me into bed in the early hours after having fallen asleep himself on the sofa.

"Daddy, Maddie at school has a new baby, and I want one too. Harry said I could have anything I wanted for my birthday, and I've decided I want a baby."

I sighed, picking him up and racing up the stairs to find my Harry elbow-deep in a pot of Bolognese sauce...with a tablet in his hand. Studying. He was preparing for his first exam in his new quest to become a qualified financial advisor—under Jane's careful tuition, of course—and cooking at the same time. And parenting. Whoever said that multitasking was hard hadn't met my Harry.

"Hi, babes," I whispered into his neck, sniffing the back of his head. He smelled of old musty shop, menswear, suits, a faint whiff off this morning's aftershave lingering. Like always.

"Hey, yourself." He smiled back, turning around to plant a kiss on my mouth. "Luca says we have to buy him a baby."

"We do, do we? And where do you buy babies, Luca?"

"I dunno. I can ask Maddie." He grinned. "Stooopid. You can't buy babies. They come out of the mummy's tummy." He rolled his eyes and ran off.

Luca was the carbon copy of Harry with the same freckled skin, blonde mop of unruly hair, thin build and full of chaotic energy. I had no doubt we'd have our work cut out raising him because the last couple of months...

What a fucking ride.

It hadn't been easy.

"How was work, clinical lead Owen Thunder?" Harry asked, finally putting his tablet down.

"All good, thank you." I grinned, ripping the hoodie over my head. "Busy. Still lots to learn."

I had *so much* to learn I didn't think it would ever end. I'd gone for a promotion in the middle of this mess, failed it, tried again, smashed it. I still had so many things to figure out, and so did Harry, because whenever the two of us thought we'd grasped something, life would always hit us straight in the face.

Like when Harry had decided to change his name to Cartwright, to finally put his past in the past and embrace the new him. That's when we'd realised that Luca's surname was still down as Thunder, and we would never be a family with all these combinations of names and stupid ideas that would never truly matter. We would always be Thunders, even me, because the guy stood there cooking our dinner was the love of my life, and family or not, I was a Thunder now. Always would be.

"I've grated a load of veg down in the sauce, and it looks rank, but Luca tried it and said it was good. Not like his gramma's, but whatever. I need to get Valerie to write down her recipe. Damn, this adulting is hard work."

"We don't need to be super healthy all the time. Social is not going to come knocking on the door just because we have greasy pizza once in a while."

"You're the nurse. You're the expert on all these things." He stuck his tongue out at me. "We'll have pizza on Friday. I'm working late. We have the Khan Industries jubilee party coming in for their final fittings. All twenty-seven of them."

"Business is booming then."

The smile on his face said it all. He knew his morning suits from his dinner jackets, his cravats from his skinny neckties. He rambled on about three-piece suits and herringbone patterns in his sleep. He could fit a top hat by eye, and he also knew how to talk to people and, as Brian had so eloquently said, could bullshit his way out of any situation. Apparently a requirement to work in high-end menswear.

There'd also been the small inconvenience of a shower-floor incident involving Brian and a broken foot, and Andrew was apparently a genius behind the scenes but hopeless on the shop floor. I still remembered that phone call like it was yesterday. Harry had worked there ever since. First for two weeks—Brian had deducted the cost of my rental suit from his first pay cheque. Harry had insisted or he'd walk away and never speak to Brian again. Then he'd signed on for another two months over summer.

Brian still fanned around him like a proud fairy godfather, and Harry put up with it but only because he now managed the corporate clients, leaving Brian to play more golf. It was a win all round, and Harry loved it. Every minute in that shop now seemed to make him happy, which hadn't always been the case at home. That was life. And life was sometimes full of bullshit and drama.

But we'd made it. I was so bloody proud of him, and of myself, because we could so easily *not* have made it.

There had been times that I didn't really want to think back to. Like the first time we got rejected by the foster-care program. I'd been on a night shift, and Harry had drunk himself into unconsciousness. When I got home, I'd made good on my threats and taken him down to A&E and had his stomach pumped.

Enough to teach us both another life lesson.

Words. Not vodka.

He'd not touched a drop since, but I got triggered by the slightest sight of a bottle of drink. Harry laughed that I couldn't even go to a supermarket without having a small panic if we walked past the hard liquor aisle.

True. But it was fine.

There had also been good days. Like the day when Harry had finally stood up to Jane and told her to back the hell off. In more eloquent words perhaps, but the meaning had been the same.

She'd gawked at him, in shock for a minute or two. Then she'd embraced him and told him she'd never thought he would, how proud she was of him. How he was a bloody fighter and now—now he was ready. *Go get 'em*, she'd said. *Grab them by the horns. You've got this.*

Jane had gone to court with Harry and held his hand as his mum was handed a massive fine for tax evasion. The former Mrs Thunder had skulked back to Tenerife without even a word to her son. Jane was also the one who'd held him afterwards and told him he'd done good.

He hadn't drunk a drop. Not even wanted to.

Then we'd found out the reason we'd been rejected to take on Luca had had nothing to do with who we were and everything to do with Douglas Thunder. Because Chantal Williams had been a young girl with dreams, and Douglas Thunder had used her and crushed her and then tried to buy her off with a down payment on a house. Her parents hated the name Thunder just as much as anyone else whose life had been touched by that man. Chantal had passed away after a short, cruel, brutal illness, leaving four-year-old Luca with her distraught elderly parents. Her house had been repossessed by the bank, and Mr Williams' dementia had forced him into a home, leaving Mrs Williams struggling to care for the child in a small apartment on her own. Mrs Williams couldn't cope with a lively five-year-old and needed a hip replacement and full-time carers.

Despite that, she'd vetoed Luca ever having any contact with his father's side of the family. She'd rather he'd gone to live with strangers than live with Harry Thunder.

Harry hadn't blamed her one bit.

It had taken meetings, letters, many short, polite telephone exchanges, months of training, tears... So many fucking tears.

Mrs Williams had balls, but Harry had them too, and the fact remained that Luca was the love of her life, her beloved grandchild.

Mrs Williams now adored Harry. She called him Son. He called her Mum. We had dinner with her every Sunday night. I often brought my mum too. Sometimes we collected Mr Williams from the nursing home and took him out in the garden in his wheelchair.

Sometimes life was cruel. Other times?

We were happy. I couldn't describe it any other way.

"Andrew and Brian still want to have us over for dinner one night, but I said we'll have to get a sitter in. I'm still not happy leaving Luca with anyone else at bedtime."

"Luca will be fine. And anyway, Joe would come babysit."

"I know. But it still...it feels too new."

"It'll be fine. We need to learn to let go too."

"I don't want him to grow up. I want us to be like this, always."

"You mean broke? I paid the builders today."

"Good." He sighed, but it was a good sigh.

We were still in the same house. Our little home that now had a tiny hallway masquerading as a living room and a brand-new wall partition to create a bedroom for Luca. It was ridiculous, but it was what we could afford, and Harry's wage helped and we were...

We were OK.

"Daddy! I got another sticker at school today. And I have a new reading book!"

"No!" I boomed, picking Luca up, kissing the side of his head. "Not a sticker? How good are you? What did you do to deserve that?"

He shrugged his little shoulders and smiled. "I dunno. Mrs Patel likes me. She said I read really well."

"I know you read really well, and I can't wait for you to read to me later. Are we having another chapter of the dinosaur book before bed?"

He wriggled down from my grip, again running off. I had no doubt he would go grab his books and bring them all to the table and demand stories during dinner and all the other things he wanted.

"Good job." Harry sighed, plonking the pot down on the table. "The spaghetti is a little overcooked, but it tastes OK."

"It smells good. I'll eat it."

"I need a shower, I'm, like, covered in tomato splatters."

"Let's eat, then I'll gladly...help you shower."

"I wish." He winked.

Yeah, I did too. Something else that hadn't been covered in the foster-care manual. Sex didn't happen anymore. Apart from in the mornings after we dropped Luca at school, then we sometimes ran home and fucked like morons in the hallway before Harry had to open the shop at ten.

Life wasn't easy, but we managed. We lived. And every hurdle so far, we'd smashed it, perhaps not effortlessly and elegantly because we both carried scars, things that we'd done to each other, hurtful words neither of us meant. But we were the Thunder Boys. Owen, Harry and Luca. And who knew what the future would bring?

"So who's going to be the mummy?" Luca piped up in the doorway. "We need to find someone to be the mummy."

"For the baby?" Harry asked like this was a normal conversation.

"Yes, Daddy has to be the daddy, and then we need a mummy."

"What about me?" Harry laughed. "Do I not belong to this family?"

"Stoopid. You're Harry. You and Daddy can both be the daddies. And I will be the big brother. It's a really important job. Maddie even got a present from her new baby. An iPad. I need an iPad."

"A mummy is really important, I agree," Harry said calmly, sitting himself down as I plated up our food. "But some mummies and daddies have babies, and then they can't look after them. It's not their fault. Sometimes the mummies or daddies are sick, or maybe they are too poor to look after their babies. Sometimes they are just not the right kind of people to be a parent. There are all kinds of reasons. And then someone else has to look after the baby."

"My mummy is dead," Luca said. "And now you look after me. And Gramma."

"Exactly." Harry smiled. "There are lots of awesome people who look after babies. Families come in all shapes and sizes. It doesn't matter who you are as long as you love each other and look after each other. And remember your mummy loved you very, very much. Next time we see Gramma, we'll look at all her photos again. And you have a photo next to your bed, remember?"

"Yeah." He looked a little confused. Then smiled. "So the new baby will have to have a different mummy. Don't worry. I'll ask Mrs Patel."

"I'm not sure Mrs Patel will want to have another baby." I was trying here, though a slight panic was rising in my chest.

"Mrs Patel *loves* babies," Luca said confidently, shoving another forkful of spaghetti into his mouth. "And she's really pretty."

Harry just laughed. I did too. Yeah, this was going to be a ride all right.

"Luca, babies are a big thing. You sometimes need a mummy and a daddy to make one, that's correct. Sometimes you have different parents. Sometimes even just one parent. But look how lucky you are. You have Gramma and Granddad, who love you. And you have me. I love you."

I did. So much. Even though he was a right little shit. Just like his big brother.

"And I love you too," Harry said, "and all together, we are the Thunder Boys and we are kind of awesome. Am I right?" He always knew how to find those words. He never stopped finding them these days. Always talking. If it wasn't to Luca, he was chattering away to me, and he was always on the phone in the evening, discussing assignments and coursework with Jane. He'd also taken up art classes with Joe, and Brian was trying to get him to go back to playing golf. Apparently, he used to play. In another life.

Not that he had time for golf. He coached children's rugby with Eddie and Luca every Saturday. Well, better him than me, but it meant I was up at the crack of dawn to spend my weekend mornings on a deckchair in a muddy field shouting supportive nonsense to a bunch of kids running around. And then we'd spend Sunday shouting about all the mud on the stairs and trying to wash grass stains out of white socks.

Life. It was a full-on thing.

"Did I tell you?" Harry piped up, his mouth full of food. "Eddie and Joe finally signed up for the first adoption information briefing. I think meeting Luca here has influenced them."

"Yeah, Joe said. Those two need kids." As soon as possible because we weren't going to sit here and parent on our own. We needed dad friends. Other families like us. And Luca needed...babies.

"Am I an influencer?" Luca asked, sticking his fork carefully into his pile of spaghetti. "What's an influencer?"

"It's someone really interesting who teaches you about things." That was Harry, always on point.

"Or someone not interesting at all, who talks a load of nonsense." And me, cutting the bullshit.

"I don't get it." Luca scrunched up his nose. "I had sausages for lunch today."

Welcome to our lives.

"And Joshua stuck a pea up his nose."

Yeah. I wouldn't change it for anything. Ever.

chapter twenty four

Harry

Six months later

Every Sunday, except for this one, Luca and I walked past the site where Thunder and Lightning Ltd had once stood. The old two-storey brick buildings were no longer there, and in their place stood a gleaming bright discount supermarket.

It wasn't a walk I took by choice. Unfortunately, the road it was on led to the park where Eddie and I played rugby with Luca and his little mates. Well, we taught it. I had a hoodie saying Coach and everything, so it wasn't like I had the choice not to pass by.

My father would have turned in his grave. If he'd had one. Which was a horrible thought to think when he was there, under my feet, scattered with all his hopes and dreams.

I sometimes stopped and just stood there, wondering what he would have said to me if he'd seen me. It wouldn't have been words of kindness. I was pretty sure he would have been fuming. Looking back, I was fuming too.

"Hey, Dad," I'd whisper, looking down at the pavement. The imposing car park gleamed with brightly coloured cars. "Look, I'm happy, OK? Luca's brilliant. He's doing so well. And it doesn't fucking matter, but I'm glad you're not here anymore."

I *was* glad. Grateful that he'd had no part whatsoever in Luca's life. And then I'd cringe and shrug off the unease and hold Luca's hand and remember that some good had come from this. I had him, and he had me, and Owen was there to keep us all together.

Luca had never been alone. He'd always been safe, loved, cared for and known that things would always be OK in the end.

I was in control now, and everything would always be OK. I knew that.

I had a full-time job that I strangely enjoyed. I sometimes dealt with people who remembered who I'd once been. Fine. I'd learnt to shrug it off with a cool smile. I also dealt with people who were truly nice humans. Men wanting to dress for occasions. Men who were consumed by grief, wanting to look respectful for the funeral. Grooms wanting to look good for their wedding day. Other men wanting to look a million pounds for the woman of their dreams. Or the man of their dreams. We had quite the reputation for 'catering to the community', as Brian would say. I'd fitted humans of every shape and size, and it didn't matter what was underneath those clothes. Brian would work his magic, and I was not too cack-handed with the pin cushion myself. A nip and a tuck here and there, sizing up across the shoulders and cleverly tucking the fabric down to straighten the waist.

There were more tears in our menswear department than in the bridal shop across the road. I could tell you that.

And I was slowly getting this financial advisor stuff down. I'd resisted Jane's idea for a long time, claiming I would be the worst financial advisor ever, sitting here with my bankruptcy in my back pocket—the worst red flag in my résumé if you asked me—but I was good with numbers. I'd become good with people. It was all about logic and investing safely and not taking those huge risks. Pensions were strangely exciting. Mortgages? I was leaving those to Jane for now. Maybe one day, my own finances would be in order. That's why I was doing this, so I could learn. Become someone who wasn't terrified of my own shadow. I had a home. One day, when the bankruptcy was behind me, I would have my name on our mortgage. I had a child who depended on me not fucking up. Well, Mrs Williams would have my head on a plate if I did.

I wasn't alone, and I never would be. People had my back these days, and it was a strange feeling to know that. An even stranger one to believe in it.

But I did believe it.

It was a Sunday in late summer, and the sun was shining, streaming through the open windows into the room. The breeze was non-existent, and the oppressive heat was making me sweat in my suit.

The suit was a rental, one I'd never be able to afford to buy for myself, but it was perfect. My tie was bright green, Owen's patterned in the same shade. He was wearing neon-green trainers. I was wearing them too.

A gift from Joe and Eddie.

Those shoes had made me laugh at first. Now, though, I was almost in tears looking down at our matching feet. What the hell was it with weddings and all the crying?

All the others in the room were people who mattered. That had been my only request, and Owen had agreed. We were going to get married, then we were having a ridiculously over-the-top roast dinner at the pub next door. We would have ice cream for dessert, and the people who mattered would be there.

Luca stood next to us in his matching suit. His tie had a Pokémon pattern on it, much to Brian's disgust, but Luca had chosen it, and who were we to argue?

I smiled at Mrs Williams, dabbing her eyes, and Mr Williams in his wheelchair.

Owen's mum was wearing her best hat. I loved his mum—almost as much as I loved Owen, which made me laugh, standing there like a fool. I grabbed Owen's hand. He plucked a tissue out of his pocket and dabbed my eyes.

"Stop crying, Harry!" Luca said with a grin. "It makes you look silly."

Yeah, it did. I didn't mind.

"I'm glad you asked me to be your best man. I would have killed you if you hadn't."

That was Eddie, next to me. He wouldn't have killed me because I would always have asked him, just like he'd asked me.

Joe was next to Owen, wearing something Brian had almost had a coronary over. I loved it. The most stunning black silk jumpsuit, tucked just right at the waist. It was very much Joe. And from the way Eddie was drooling over him? Yeah. He looked good.

"Stop drooling over your husband," I whispered to Eddie.

"He's not wearing underpants. Apparently, the seams were too obvious with that fabric. Now I can't stop thinking about that little fact." Eddie laughed.

"It's my wedding." I grunted, smiling because...yeah. We talked about these things. Sometimes it was embarrassing. Other times? Eddie. Funniest man ever. And if you couldn't talk about these things with your best friend, then they were not your best friend.

"I'm so sorry." That was the officiant, rushing into the room. "The traffic was bad, and I got a little lost."

Not that we'd been waiting long. I'd waited all my life to figure this out. Love. Life. Marriage. Here I was. Getting married. I could wait a few more minutes.

"I'm so sorry," she said again, dropping the folder she'd fished out of her bag all over the floor. "Oh, God." Papers everywhere. With an embarrassed smile, she straightened up, carefully putting everything back in the folder.

I glanced behind me. Everyone who mattered was in this room. The people who loved me. The people who'd shaped me. And the people who were *not* here? I didn't need them anymore.

"You wrote your own vows, so I will let you speak. Owen, will you go first?"

I'd been so deep in thought, I'd missed the start of my own wedding, but now I was back in the room with a bang, my heart beating out of my chest as Owen took my hands.

"I'll keep this short because there are just a few words I want to say. You know them anyway because you helped me put them together." He smiled. I smiled too. Somewhere in the background, Maggie blew her nose. She mouthed *sorry* to me as I grinned in her direction.

"Harry. When we first met, we were both bad with our words. I was scared of saying them. You? I think you'd forgotten how to use them. And somehow, we still managed to string our sentences together. In a way, that was the inevitable outcome. The two of us were always meant to be. And that is why I'm standing here today. I'll always be here. And I'll always use my words. You're the centre of my world, and in return, I'll be the centre of yours. If you fall, I'll catch you. If I fall, I know you'll catch me too. Harry, I love you, and I will love you. Always."

He was just there. In my space. Holding my hands as my heart beat, now slow and steady because I was his and he was mine. And we'd always been good at this. Being us. Calming. Safe. And now, when it was my turn to speak, I just smiled.

"Owen, you are the first person I fell in love with because before I met you, I didn't really understand what it meant to belong to someone else. Love can be many things. It can be silly. Ridiculous. Stupid. Frightening. Sometimes even downright dirty. And it can also be really, really simple. I love you, and it's so easy to love you because you love me too. That is what I hope we always remember. That the small things in life are what matter, and as long as we have each other? There will be love. The good kind of love." I had to stop. Laugh out loud.

"I love you. I promise I'll always say those three words to you. And when times get hard, I'll say them again. That's my promise to you. I'll go to sleep every night with your hand in mine. Then I'll say them. And I'll wake up in the morning and kiss your stupid face. And then I'll no doubt say them again."

I was still laughing, and so was he. And his face was stupid, all scrunched up with emotion.

I was good at this public talking thing, apparently. I hadn't meant to say it like that, but then, I was me. And he was Owen, and now we were supposed to kiss.

"She said kiss!" Luca shouted. "You need to kiss or we'll be late for lunch!"

"Yes!" Owen's mum laughed. "You tell them, Luca! There's a good roast dinner waiting for us next door!"

This wedding was out of control, and I didn't even have a ring on my finger.

"The rings! Oh God. I forgot the rings!" The officiant was almost in tears herself, flipping through the pages of her folder.

"I'll do them!" Luca shouted. He already had them on his fingers, Owen's on one hand and mine on the other.

"Daddy, this one is yours. No stop! Wrong! I forgot. You get Harry's, and you have to stick it on his finger."

"Like this?" Owen joked, holding it over my thumb.

"No, stooopid. Properly. We practised? Remember?"

They had. I'd practised too.

He grabbed my hand, my Owen, and he carefully slid my ring over my finger. A plain silver band. We'd chosen them.

"Hello, husband," he whispered.

"Hello, yourself," I whispered back.

"Harry, your turn. This one goes on Daddy's finger. OK? Do you need me to help you?"

Apparently, I did, as Luca shoved the ring onto Owen's finger. I helped. A little.

"Now you can kiss." Luca would one day make a fine officiant, although the officiant we had was now laughing along. Madness. But very much our madness.

Eddie smiled. "Best wedding ever."

"Good job, Luca," Joe said, patting him on the head. Luca looking very pleased with himself.

So, then we did. I put my arms around my man, and we kissed. And he was smiling against my lips, and I was laughing as he pulled back, took my face between his hands, and then he kissed me again.

"You're going to be trouble, aren't you?" he said. "It was bad enough when you were my secret little crush. Then you became my boyfriend, and now I've married you. What on earth was I thinking?"

"No idea. Did I just marry a bloke? Eddie, help me here!" I laughed.

"Idiot." Owen grinned.

"Yeah. No help for this guy. Says he's not even gay." Now I hated Eddie.

"I know!" Joe squealed. "The wedding night should be interesting."

"Shut up." I groaned. "There are innocent children in the room."

"To the gorgeous grooms!" That was Owen's mum.

"To Harry and Owen!" And Joe's dad, tears in his eyes, Jane clapping vigorously beside him.

"Now where's this roast dinner we've been promised?" Maggie. Hugging me and patting my cheek.

This wedding had gone to hell. We were supposed to walk out to some stupid piece of music. Instead, we were all standing here surrounded by people, laughter ringing through the air. Luca was showing the officiant his tie, and Owen put his arms around me, and Joe was giggling, and Brian was fussing over my collar...

And then we lived happily ever after.

Nah. We went to lunch. Then we played football in the pub garden, and I got grass stains on my suit trousers and things just were.

Because this was our wedding, and I wouldn't have wanted it any other way.

The End

acknowledgements

Thank you to my amazing team of humans who make my stories the best they can be. You know who you are. Debbie McGowan for the brilliant edits, and for being so incredibly patient with my messy, messy men. Sarah Coppin at Manor Editing Services for picking up on all my little mistakes.

Special thank you to the lovely Rourke for again helping me create the perfect cover.

Massive gratitude to the Thunder and Lightning team on Discord, who beta read this and came up with solutions to my many ridiculous plot holes. Special mention to Moopaloop who named Joe for me.

about the author

Sophia Soames should be old enough to know better but has barely grown up. She has been known to fangirl over TV shows, has fallen in and out of love with more pop stars than she dares to remember, and has a ridiculously high-flying (un-)glamourous real-life job.

Her long-suffering husband just laughs at her antics. Their children are feral. The dogs are too.

She lives in a creaky old house in rural London, although her heart is still in her native Scandinavia.

Discovering that the stories in her head make sense when written down has been part of the most hilarious midlife crisis ever, and she hopes it may long continue.

Also by Sophia Soames

717 Miles

717 Miles Christmas

The Scandinavian Comfort Series

Little Harbour

Open Water

Baking Battles

In this Bed of Snowflakes We Lie

The Naked Cleaner

The Chistleworth series

Custard and Kisses

Ship of Fools

This Thing with Charlie

The London Love Series

BREATHE

EXHALE

TASTE

Force Majeure

Dirty Sexy Stupid Love

White Noise

With Magdalena di Sotru

Life is Good and Other Lies

Life is Right Here

Printed in Great Britain
by Amazon

0be45c06-9e98-485d-bfab-8c2d554de3c9R01